CASCADIA SUBDUCTION SHIFT

1366Books

Ontario

Canada

ONTARIO ARTS COUNCIL
CONSEIL DES ARTS DE L'ONTARIO
an Ontario government agency
un organisme du gouvernement de l'Ontario

Canada Council for the Arts
Conseil des arts du Canada

CASCADIA SUBDUCTION SHIFT

Fictions

BRIAN KAUFMAN

1366Books

An imprint of Guernica Editions

Guernica founder: Antonio D'Alfonso
General editor: Michael Mirolla
1366 Books editor: Stuart Ross
Interior design & typesetting: Stuart Ross
Cover & 1366 logo design: Underline Studio
Author photo: Columpa C Bobb

Guernica Editions Inc.
1241 Marble Rock Rd., Gananoque, ON K7G 2V4
2250 Military Road, Tonawanda, NY 14150-6000 USA
www.guernicaeditions.com

Distributors:
Independent Publishers Group (IPG), 600 North Pulaski Rd., Chicago, IL 60624
University of Toronto Press Distribution (UTP), 5201 Dufferin St.,
Toronto, Ontario M3H 5T8

First edition. Printed in Canada.

Library of Congress Control Number: 2026939325
Library and Archives Canada Cataloguing in Publication
Title: Cascadia subduction shift / Brian Kaufman.
Names: Kaufman, Brian, 1956- author.
Description: First edition. | Series statement: 1366Books ; 6
Identifiers: Canadiana (print) 20260171255 | Canadiana (ebook) 2026017131X | ISBN 9781778490644 (softcover) | ISBN 9781778490651 (EPUB)
Subjects: LCGFT: Autobiographical fiction. | LCGFT: Novels.
Classification: LCC PS8571.A893 C37 2026 | DDC C813/.54—dc23

For all the small fish,
the ones that fit through the net.

"Let it be therefore understood that the facts were what I say they were, but the interpretation that I give them is what I am—now."

—Jean Genet, *The Thief's Journal*

Contents

Two

SEISMIC SHIFTS

One

EARLY WARNING SIGNS

Cascadia Subduction Shift

The students had just completed a review of the eight and nine times tables and were now ardently focused on colouring in the geography project on the Pacific Northwest. The teacher, Miss Simpson, adjusted her cardigan, pulling it tighter around her shoulders on this cool November day, wet and dreary, dark even for Vancouver in the fall. It would soon be noon and lunches would come out of paper bags, battered Tupperware containers, and metal and plastic lunch boxes, filling the room, as always, with the odours of peanut butter, tuna, cheese, and curry. Miss Simpson took this opportunity of relative peace and calm to clean the chalkboards and paused to notice how the brush seemed more efficient in cool, damp weather. As she swiped the brush up and down across the board, she tended to hum to herself. But today, for no reason clear to her, she said out loud: "Many of you will likely die in the Cascadia subduction shift of 2028, when the Pacific tectonic plate will slide, diving down like a huge whale, taking the seabed with it." Then the room fell silent again and only the sound of pencils on paper could be heard. One of the children began softly humming "The Farmer in the Dell." Miss Simpson felt a sudden surge of pride, realizing she had combined, in one lesson, arithmetic, geography, geology, *and* eschatology.

Secret Doctor

He is perhaps five or six years old and being dragged along on an appointment with his mother and older sister. They are down Kingsway, near the 2400 Motel; across the street, the houses and other buildings are on a rise and set back from the road. They have to climb a flight of concrete steps to reach the sidewalk leading to the building. They are going to "see the doctor," but he can't figure out why they are not going to Dr. Williams, their family doctor, whose office is further east on Kingsway, near Joyce, across from Carlton Elementary School, the oldest school in Vancouver, founded in 1896. He recalls the portal window on the door to this other doctor's office; he'd never seen a door with a round window. There is also the smell of antiseptic. They sit in a small waiting room, sunlight beaming through the skylight onto a table with neatly arranged piles of magazines—*Maclean's, LIFE,* and *TV Guide*. The doctor—who is not Dr. Williams—steps out from an adjacent room, smiles, and says, "C'mon in, Cynthia," and his sister gets up, then turns to his mother. "Come with me," she says, but his mother doesn't rise, instead biting her lip and gesturing with her hand. "You go on," she says. "I'll be right here." And off goes his older sister, off into the other room with the "secret doctor."

The Church

He felt it every time he passed the building. A tightness in his chest, a shortness of breath. What was it with the place? Its vibe was low but palpable, oozing out toward the sidewalk, changing the air. It smelled like lost hope, stale crackers. He thought maybe…maybe it was just his haphephobia rearing its gnarly head, but he doubted it, since sports were helping him with that issue and a team hug at the end of a good game was almost tolerable. It could be the homilphobia, which was definitely worsening, and the merest belch of a pipe organ could send him into straits of panic. And the staurophobia could not be discounted, the outlines of the crosses searing their way through the walls like acid-burned etchings. Or was it the priest—a little pulse of hierophobia pushing through? Maybe. Understandable. There were stories circulating about priests at Mount Cashel out east, and other places, stories about priests doing nasty things to young boys his age. But still, this creeping terror seemed to be rooted in something—*somewhere*—else. His instincts told him it was linked to his hylophobia, because that is where it had first occurred.

Hornets

They are roaming the woods of southeast Vancouver when they see it. Hanging from the branch of a maple, it looks like a chunk of cloth, or a plastic bag snagged in the tree. Liam, the taller of the two boys, grabs a piece of rotten branch from the forest floor and hurls it at the mystery object, tearing a gaping hole in one side of the balloon-shaped grey mass. Within seconds the air is filled with hundreds of furious stinging insects—specifically, hornets. They descend with a precision wrath unknown to the two eight-year-old boys who now have nothing in mind but flight—down paths, through brush, ducking low-hanging branches, toward the fringes of the familiar bush and hopeful escape. Ten seconds into their flight, Calvin, the smaller of the two boys, catches the toe of his Converse low top on the exposed root of a massive conifer and is catapulted through the air to land rag-doll prone on the mulchy forest floor. Then they are on him—face, neck, arms, ankles—any exposed flesh, all is game. He is the enemy and is dealt with accordingly. He is stung repeatedly, mission accomplished, lessons dispatched through pain and suffering. He tries his best to pull them off, swat them away, but they've firmly inserted their tarsal claws in the cotton weave of his socks, his T-shirt. He tears at them, but there are too many. Howling and running is the only option, and young Calvin complies. His next memory is of lying on Liam's mother's bed as she puts cool, soothing cream on the dozens of stings. Like some Nordic nurse, surrounded by an angelic glow, she is radiant in her kindness.

The Well

The entranceway is a two-foot-square piece of plywood set flush into the ground. Right behind his house, Mike Moscovitch's house, just outside the basement door. When they pull the hatch lid, they find themselves staring down into a dark well, ladder rungs made from two-by-fours lining one side of the shaft. Mike looks at Ryan Adler, looks him right in the eye, and says, "See, I told you so. My dad built it, in case they drop the bomb." Ryan asks Mike if he's ever been down, and Mike says he has, but Ryan senses that his friend is lying; his top lip always quivers when he lies, and it is trembling now. Mike kneels, holding the hatch open, and says, "So? You wanna go down?" Ryan doesn't want to descend into the dark tunnel. He is afraid, and a surge of fear is making him feel cold. But still he says, "Yeah, I wanna see it." Down they go, single file, rung by rung, into the damp, the utter dark of the earth. About six feet straight down, Mike, who is below Ryan and moving slower with each rung, begins whimpering, and sputters out, "I've never been down here! My dad told me to stay out." Ryan looks up the shaft at the square of light above them. He hears voices. Then it gets dimmer and, finally, it gets dark, pitch dark as the hatch closes above them.

Crosswalk

"You either get past it or you spend the rest of your days staring into space." She realized this to be true as she stared at the still surface of her milky tea. But knowing it and saying it in her head did very little to free her of the grief that had gripped her like a straitjacket since the day her seven-year-old boy had been struck by a car in the crosswalk outside of his elementary school and sent seventy feet through the air to his—she was informed—"instant death." It meant very little that her neighbour Isabel had said these words to her out of compassion, had reached out in an effort to save her from the abyss of grief or, worse, the dark cellar of madness that she could sense, could feel, could almost see just beyond the steps that led from the kitchen down to the basement. They—the words—did nothing to erase the hole at the centre of her being, nothing to erase the memory of the phone ringing, of the sirens, of the solemn, tear-streaked faces moving toward her behind outstretched arms, the whispering voices: "Sadie, Sadie, Sadie… Oh, Sadie…" No, the words were not strong enough to erase the images, not strong enough to stretch seventy feet. Seventy. Seventy feet was a lifetime away.

Mad Bull

When Frank was a kid of maybe six or seven, his dad would take him on runs to the Burns Food plant on Powell Street. It used to stand down near Rogers Sugar Refinery, along the industrial wasteland north of the rail yards. Frank loved going on these jaunts. He and his father in the Econoline van—he'd sit centre on the engine cover, where it was warm—no seat belt or even a thought of seat belts back then. His dad working the gears, "three on the tree," as they drifted down Rupert Street to Kingsway, then west to Victoria, coasting around the corner, carrying on north past Hendry Park to Commercial Drive, and on and over the Grandview Cut. Then the slow stop-and-go along the Drive, jaywalkers scooting into traffic from First Avenue to Venables, then the curve past East Georgia, Adanac, Pender, to Hastings, and on through the rumoured "bad area" of Franklin and Pandora Streets. Then they'd hit Powell and its smells of rendering plants, chicken slaughter, fish processing. The noise of railcars being shunted in the transfer yard, squealing and squeaking, the bumpity-bump over the tracks and into guarded yards, security gates swinging open, window down, and a nod or a "Hey, Harry..." as they passed the checkpoint, the Dickensian, soot-covered sugar refinery looming to the west, just outside the windshield, and Frank tried to imagine what went on in there, what gaunt, grey-skinned workers shuffled through the sugar-dust air, what conveyor belt system moved the white gold from area to area, all hidden behind those impenetrably grimy windows, and off to his right, the towers of the Alberta Wheat Pool—concrete plinths soaring up to meet the pigeon-grey sky as the Econoline moved down the entrance road toward the plant. Frank loved the feeling of accessing secured places secreted away on the waterfront, and he realized he had the key, the password, the in, and the "in" was his dad, and in this moment of boyhood joy he also felt intense affection for his father, and he wondered, *Does he know it?* They got out of the van and headed up a short flight of wooden steps leading to the loading dock and into the warehouse area. And there, just at the entrance, stood the huge ammonia tank, an upended humpback whale—black, but the top quarter was coated in thick ice, like white lava working its way down the length of the tank. He could smell it—the ammonia—and his dad directed him around and away: "C'mon, don't stand there!" And there were noises, an amalgam of industrial strains: refrigeration fans, whining generators, squeaky pulleys, gears, whirring, hissing, squealing. Hums from indefinable sources. Now they were in the plant, fabled in his mind: the killing floor, the stun guns, the place where the mythical "crazed bull" had fled after its executioner missed his mark, only grazing the skull of the beast with his sledgehammer, sending the roaring bull for the nearest window—*Go to the light!* Then the ethereal drop of a full two storeys, crashing onto the loading dock below, only to rise and run—*Away, away, away*—from the carnage, the madness, the moaning, the lowing and crying of its mates.

Seven Seconds

He remembers November 22 as a sunny, clear day. But knowing the tricks that memory can play, he questions his recollection. Compound that with the weather statistics for Vancouver and there would be a 71 per cent chance that it had, in fact, been overcast and possibly even raining on that day. Regardless, he recalls that on a November day in 1963, he and his classmates had been sent home early from school, about two hours early, because the president of the United States had been shot. He also knows for a fact—or a maligned memory lapse—that they left the school, single file, via the side entrance, as if the school were under threat. And he remembers the sky was blue and the light was bright and they—he and his classmates—moved silently along the concrete pathway that led from the playground to Old D'oman Road and north away from the school and into their safe neighbourhood of quiet suburban homes. He and his good friend Randy walked the streets and alleyways that took them to Randy's house, wherein his mother sat weeping at the kitchen table. It wasn't until the next day that he learned that a man named Ozwad had pulled the trigger of the gun that had killed the president of the United States and had caused Randy's mom to sit at her kitchen table and weep as if enduring the death of one of her own children. Many years later he read that this day in November 1963—this exact event—had been referred to by an acclaimed American novelist as the "seven seconds that broke the back of the American century." But to him it has always been just that day in Grade 2 when they all got sent home early from school.

Small Feet, Short Legs

He'd had them his whole life: small feet and short legs. When he was young it wasn't such a big deal—all his peers had them too. It was only later that he realized something was amiss. It was around the time that one of the Thomson brothers called to him from their stoop as he passed—"Hey! When you gonna grow?" It wasn't a friendly comment of concern, as if a loved one were wondering if you were, perhaps, afflicted by dwarfism or some other malady or disorder—progeria, perhaps—but one of ridicule, derision, harassment. It was passed off as badinage, but it was a thin and transparent onion skin over the real bullying intent of their after-school diversions. The seed had been planted, and weedlike tentacles snaked out in every direction. After years of not finding shoes in his size and needing every single pair of pants altered, tailored, made to measure, he came to realize there was a vast conspiracy against him and his ilk and any others who were "out of the norm." And, once realizing that the vast conspiracy existed and obviously had many, many operatives to keep it functioning, he also realized he knew what they looked like, and that made him want to set fire to the Thomson house and all who slept there. But he didn't do it, didn't set fire to the house, because Mrs. Thomson, unlike her sons, was a very pleasant person.

Flame On

It was raining and the woods were quiet. Two of them sat high in the air on the floorboards of the unfinished tree fort. Another sat on a branch a few feet below, and when Eugene Balzar entered the clearing beneath them, the other three froze and there was no sound beyond that of the dripping rain. Balzar stood, looking around, as if perhaps he were expecting someone, or waiting for something. So when Wild Bob popped the spout on his can of Ronson lighter fluid and sent a long, arcing stream down onto the back of Balzar's new winter jacket, the other two were not surprised. After all, Wild Bob had earned his moniker honestly, through insane acts of daring. The stream shot down, looking not unlike a long jettison of urine, and was not felt or acknowledged through the back of Balzar's "Eskimo" jacket. What was surprising was the *whoosh* that followed after Wild Bob took a final drag on his Export A and flicked the burning butt downward. The fuzzy exterior of Balzar's jacket burst into a rolling orange-and-yellow ghost that moved up his back and over his head. He flapped his arms and then ran off through the woods, screaming. The two on the fort deck looked at each other with widened eyes. Wild Bob looked up at them, smirked, shot a stream of watery saliva out between his front teeth, and said, "Cool."

Dumpster Messiah

He comes at them like a shaman, a fallen god, a dumpster messiah. Thick, sore-looking red feet with big fat toes. His head too large for his body and hair thick, tangled, matted. A castaway in South Vancouver in the summer of 1968, the year of "Lady Madonna," when everyone said, "Listen to the voice, you can tell, it's the fake Paul!" He would show up—sometimes behind the school, or in the bush nearby, where they hung out. He would stare at them, just stand there smiling and staring. Barry Knowlton told him to fuck off or he'd smash his head in, but the guy didn't move, grinning like he knew something they didn't. Someone said he had escaped from Riverview, a mental institution; others said he was mentally disabled, mute, a ward of the state. It was rumoured he was building a log cabin in the woods, and one day later that summer, when it was all over, they came upon the start of a cabin. He'd made it about three feet high before being forced to abandon his project. They shuddered when they realized that meant he had an axe or, at the very least, a hatchet. But, for the most part, this silent holy man was nothing to worry about, an entertaining diversion during their summer of Grade 6. Until that day in late July or early August, when it was so quiet, still, thick heat, grasshoppers in dry grass, garter snakes squashed on the road, most of their friends away on holiday at the lake or the cabin. There were four or five of them, behind the school, smoking cigs and playing Knock Out—where you hold your breath while the other person presses their thumbs against both sides of your neck, just below your ears, until you black out. He appeared from the dark shadows of the covered patio and stood there, grinning and staring as usual, but this time something was different. One of them said, "Holy shit!" and pointed, then the others saw it too. Like a geoduck hanging from his pants, dangling halfway down his thigh. And that was it, his fatal flaw, his undoing, the beginning of this messiah's persecution. Someone must have mentioned it to their parents: it wasn't Dickie, wasn't Barry, wasn't Ronnie... Maybe Wayne, he had a strange, communicative relationship with his parents. But the Shaman of Cook Bush was never seen again. Vanished. Scooped in the night? Perhaps. Rounded up and returned to where it was he had come from, the only reminder being the partially built cabin in the woods that they would stumble upon now and then—a dream, dashed, as so many had been before.

A Really Big SHOE!

They're eating a dinner of ham, roast pork, mashed potatoes, corn, peas that look like they've been boiled for a week, and carrots you can cut with the tine of your fork. All of it circulating clockwise through a miasma of cigarette smoke. Steam pipes from the frenetic pressure cooker while *I Love Lucy* blares from the living room. The Surgeon General has yet to break from his busy holiday at the ski lodge to show us the horror face of mouth cancer, an emphysemic lung sac, or a smoker's purple leathery heart. North America still revs on car fumes and pork bellies. Be happy! Everyone sucking madly, a last drag or two before stubbing them out in the overflowing ashtray, tucking into the grub. Everyone except Henry—"Ma! I don't have a knife!" Henry's the youngest, still pretending he doesn't smoke. But there's a pack of Export A's wedged in his jean jacket pocket that he gets from the gas station using a fake "parental approval letter":

> *To Whom It May Concern:*
> *Please allow my son, Henry, to purchase a pack of Export A's on my behalf.*
> *Sincerely yours,*
> *Mrs. I. Koop*

The ink is faded, the paper fuzzy along the fold lines, but it always works. What the hell does the gas jockey/grease monkey care? Henry and his pal Bibs tuck out back the station, rip off the Cellophane wrapper, pop the pack—that smell!—keep the flavour-protective foil, 'cause later they'll burn the paper backing off and burnish the foil to the pack. Cool. They boost themselves up and into the cinder-block enclosure the station has for discarded tires and lounge back on the spongy stacks, breathe in the summer smells of oil and rubber and grease. They're hobo kings of the tire heap—yeah! The family wraps up dinner—the old man swabbing the gravy dregs with a folded slab of Wonder Bread—and votes are cast for dessert: 3 for Jell-O; 2 for rice pudding. The old man and older brother just back from their October hunting/slaughter trip. No moose luck, instead unlucky deer luck hangs in the garage by a meat hook, fluids draining from its snout like thick red lacquer, soaking the sawdust spill below. Tonight they will watch (along with 73 million other North American viewers) *The Ed Sullivan Show*. Henry is crammed on the couch with his mother and sister, brother on the orange-sherbet loveseat, Pops in the La-Z-Boy with a shot of whisky and a smoke, keeping an open mind to what is about to erupt from the screen of the black-and-white Fleetwood Stereo Console. Ed does his half spin, raises his left arm: "And now, something for the youngsters. Direct from Liverpool, England—THE BEATLES!" Squeals erupt as the Fab Four launch into "She Loves You." Henry has drum practice before bed, once or twice through the Ventures' "Walk Don't Run." Lessons are Tuesdays and Thursdays, where he will stumble-drum to records on the player while his instructor blows smoke rings at the ceiling. *"More wrist!"* he will yell. *"More WRIST!"*

Fight

The Auster brothers exit the King Joy grocery store just as the five of them approach. There is nowhere for the brothers to go, given the timing of departures and arrivals. Immediate pushing and shoving begins. Someone says to the older brother, Devon, "*You*, fight him!" and points at one of the biggest boys from the group of five. Devon says, "I won't fight him, but I'll fight *him*!" and points at the smallest one in the group. Whoops go up and the shoving starts. A couple of weak, small-fisted punches are thrown, and soon they are clasped together in headlocks, twisting and pulling, gravel crunching beneath their runners, and then they fall—sideways—crash hard to the ground, strain and squirm to be on top. Light punches to each other's heads and then a loud scream erupts, a yell in the small boy's ear, and he knows something bad has happened. Devon is howling, crying, and his smaller brother tries to jump in to help, and one of the other five boys turns and punches the younger Auster brother—Allan—in the face, and he falls back against a low wooden fence, slides to the ground as Devon rolls away, holding his head, hands cupped over his ears. And then again, due to timings of arrivals, the much older brother of the Auster boys rounds the corner with a couple of his rebel friends. "Hey!" they hear. Then dispersion, chaos, panic ensues as the group of five scatter. The older brother and his two friends pursue them like guard dogs—across streets, across lawns, down alleys. The five are soon separated and the smallest takes desperate refuge over a fence and to the back door of a darkened house. He knocks—*bangs*—but the door does not open. There is no response to his panicked pounding. Trapped and facing his fate under the boots and blows of three teenage greasers—they, oddly, open a door for his escape: "Who kicked Devon in the head?" They approach the bottom of the steps. "Tell us or you're dead." "Nietzsche," he says. "Friedrich Nietzsche." They seem to accept this without question, and so much has already been blamed on Nietzsche that he doesn't feel bad at all about saying it.

Flying Squirrels

By the end of their effort, there were ten, maybe twelve, kids gripping and dangling from the long rope swing that was strung between two massive Douglas firs. It had started with Brett Sanderson, easing off from the launch platform—a sheet of three-quarter-inch plywood nailed to the top of a twelve-foot-high stump. With each successive arc of the swing, another daredevil would make the jump, leap from the platform toward the approaching swing, now carrying an additional body. They would grab the rope and settle into a spot upon Brett's lap, which in turn rested upon an oval plywood disc, which itself sat upon a huge knot—the size of a large cantaloupe—made by tying the ends of the two descending jute ropes that comprised the swing. Back and forth they swung, powered by gravity, inertia, kinetic energy, each arc forward getting lower and each trip back toward the platform making the leap to the swing that much further. "Do it!" and "You can make it!" ringing out through the woods as the next jumper paused, stuttered on top of the platform, sometimes letting the human pendulum swing away, only to add more danger and terror to its next return. Wild Bob had waited until all the others had jumped. Now the pendulum was slowing, and the call went out—"JUMP!"—and he did. Not unlike a flying squirrel, he sailed, arms and legs spread, then down, grabbing the back of someone's jacket, from which he dangled six feet above the ground, while the cheers roared—*"YES! YES!"* Brett now screaming that he couldn't feel his legs and they all had to *"Get off! Get off now!"* The day became one of legend. At school, around the playground, the story circulated and, of course, grew. By the end of the following week, the story was told how Wild Bob had jumped fifteen feet! *Fifteen feet* and made it!

Gasoline

Doman Street—or, as they had always referred to it, "Old Doman Road"—ran south along the west side of their elementary school. It officially ended at the south boundary of the school property but actually continued down into the bush to the city dump and was used as a "service road" by city workers. It was also used as access to the deeper reaches of the bush between one of the most remote stops on the Vancouver bus system (54th Avenue and Doman Road) and the city dump. This road led to secret spots, teen hangouts for drinking, campfires, tree forts, the resting spot for numerous abandoned cars, and an area to squat for homeless men (still referred to as "hobos"), many of whom were shell-shocked WWII veterans. It was a would-be Lover's Lane from a David Lynch film, all worldly beauty shrivelling under a haze of suppressed violence and twisted lust. At the age of ten or eleven they roamed the bush like proud archaeologists of some debased, primal society: rain-drenched skin mags, empty mickey bottles—labels peeled and fading—flattened Old Style beer cases, used condoms, smoke packs, and the occasional pair of underwear—the crude evidence of teenage misadventure. They found several cars, most likely stolen, driven as far into the bush as could be managed, stripped of any useful parts, seats often torn, sometimes gone altogether. The boys would sit there, pretend driving, smoking cigarettes, dreaming of a future populated with hot rods—souped-up Chevys and cut-frame vans. One of these cars, flat on the ground, wheels gone, also had a missing gas cap. One of the boys produced a box of Firebird wooden matches, and the dare went out. Who would toss the match? Wild Bob was always up for feats of risk and danger. He got close, peered into his own fiery fantasy, and struck the match with a sharp draw against the underside of his jeans. He looked at them, then tossed it in. *Whoosh!* A jet of blue-and-orange flame shot out of the spout, and Bob leap-frogged backwards, standing erect. He no longer had eyebrows or eyelashes. Maniacal laughter filled the air, as if they were on the uninhabited island with Ralph, Jack, and Piggy. It was then that they realized they lived in a world of unknown wonders.

Ponies

They were deep in the woods when they found it. A squatter's shack—but they didn't know that then, they were only twelve years old—made from scrap plywood. They snapped the combination lock with ease and swung open the door. They thought they had found a teen hideout, a fort that would yield a trove of bounty—comic books, beer, smokes, skin mags. But as they stepped inside, a silence fell upon them. Instead of a fort littered with candy wrappers, pop cans, and the secret refuse of pimple-faced boys, they were stunned by a scene of pristine domesticity: a prospector's cot that was neatly made; a small wooden counter held a propane camp stove, a coffee pot, a coffee cup, and a drinking glass placed to dry on a folded tea towel. And the walls—the rough-surfaced plywood walls—were covered with pictures of ponies and horses, torn from magazines and stapled in place. A scene of rural simplicity surrounded the boys. They stared and gazed around the room and then at each other. The silence was thick. They backed out slowly, each guilty in his private sin of invasion. No one had to tell them that what they had done was wrong; it screamed at them from every direction of the surrounding woods. They closed the door and reset the clasp as best they could, then hung the broken lock from the bent clasp and turned to walk away. Now the little fence of branches and small tree trunks that surrounded the shack made sense. Of course. It was a corral, a corral to keep the ponies in.

Venting

It wasn't actually a cave, but they did descend. Further south from the tar pits of the city dump, an elevated area overlooked the Fraser River, and out of it rose three leaning concrete columns. Frank and Wild Bob had no idea what the columns were, what their purpose was; they were just another mystery among many that the two friends explored. What they actually were was venting tubes, hollow and sunk in the ground deep enough to allow excess methane—and other gases produced in the decomposition of organic matter—to escape. Wild Bob and Frank hoisted themselves up over the lip to peer in; what the smell was, who knew? Inside, rebar handles served as a ladder leading down, but for what purpose? Maintenance? More likely for a worker to descend and take gas measurements. But to the eyes of two twelve-year-old boys, it was the Temptation of Christ all over again. Down they went, rung after rung, until they had descended fifteen feet. They perched there like sparrows, one above the other. And then—*from where do the ideas of young boys erupt?*—they decided to have a smoke. A single came out of a shirt pocket and a Ronson lighter from the back pocket of Wild Bob's Wrangler jeans. The flip of the lid...the rasp of the flint, and...somehow, no explosion. Wild Bob lit the cig, took a drag, smiled up at Frank, and handed him the smoke. Why they weren't shot out of the tube like two circus clowns is a mystery best left for wiser, inquiring minds. It has been said that God protects children and idiots, so they had a double count going for them. They shared a few more drags on the hot cigarette, then climbed, slowly, back toward the light.

Silver Dollar

He was throwing a baseball back and forth with his friend Ron Wolanski when a toss cleared his mitt and sailed into the neighbour's yard. He scrambled up the horizontal slats and vaulted the top, launching himself into the yard. He was crossing the lawn to the ball when she attacked, grabbing a clump of his hair from behind, wrapping it twice around her index finger and yanking. He thumped to the grass as a huge tuft of hair was removed from the back of his head, a bald patch the size of a silver dollar now appearing at his crown. Even at eight years old, he knew that the rage unleashed on him that day had little to do with the baseball that sailed over the fence into her yard—it was years of pent-up hate that fuelled the sudden and vicious attack. Out of nowhere she had bolted, like a guard dog: Audrey Denfield. She had always despised him, sought to inflict not pain but *humiliation* upon him. Humiliation, the queen of revenge. Lasts longer than pain and burns deeper. And her opportunity had presented itself; she could not—and *did not*—fail to seize the moment. Dickie Swisdale had to go to school the next day with a massive bald spot at the back of his head. He knew he would be ridiculed, taunted, laughed at—and he was. He attempted to camouflage the shame with a criss-cross of two small Band-Aids, and when the teacher, Miss Neudork, asked him, "Richard, what happened to your head?" he told her he had cut himself. And when she hovered above him as he sat at his desk and asked him softly if she could "take a look," he froze, didn't know what to do. Then she ever so gently pulled aside the edge of one Band-Aid, said, "I see…" and Dickie sighed, thinking she would push the edge of the bandage down, sealing his secret beneath. But instead she pulled it back completely and announced: “Look, class, Richard is losing his hair!” Laughter erupted around him. Kids pointed. He could feel his face burning, turning red, and that was when he realized that Audrey Denfield had won. For now.

The Janitor

We steal three cigarettes from my mom's pack of Number 7s and climb onto the roof of the school. It is ungodly hot. We squat against the exterior wall of the gym and squint south toward the Fraser River. Stiles flips the lid on his Zippo, ignites a floppy flame, and leans in, head sideways, and puffs—one, two, three times—before he gets it. He extends the flame, goes into a hacking fit, and drops the lighter to the gravel. I grab it up, hold my smoke like Colonel Klink on *Hogan's Heroes,* and raise the flame to the end. We puff and cough, marvelling at the mix of smoke and heat, then Stiles says, "Walker's old man got mouth cancer and they cut his voice box out… Talks through a hole in his throat now." "Castro's been smoking cigars since he was ten," I say, "and he's still alive." Stiles is about to say something else, maybe that Castro is dead or more about Walker's dad, but his jaw just drops and hangs, a wisp of smoke drifting out. Then I see him too—the guy—all in white and a straw hat, like some dude from Florida. Stiles's foot slides in the gravel like he wants to get up and run, but we're too dizzy to even stand, and the big guy has reached us anyway. "Hi, boys," he says, puffing, out of breath. "What a fine day for a sit in the sun and a sweet, slow smoke." Stiles gives me a glance that says, *He touches us, we pull our knives.* I look at Mr. Florida's feet, his weird sandals of rope and tire rubber. We're down to the last third of our smokes, and everything suddenly feels hotter. Florida Guy points and says, "Wouldn't happen to have an extra one of those, would you? It's been seven years since I last had a cigarette, but that's going to change today." Stiles's eyes widen and stare, and I offer our third, unlit smoke to Florida Guy. "Here," I say, "we got one left." He takes the cigarette, runs his tubular fingers down the length of it. "A marvel, really," he says. "Such ingenuity...such flare." Stiles offers up the Zippo, but Florida waves it off. "Thank you, son, but no...I think I shall savour it a spell...and there is plenty of fire where I'm going. It is such fortune that I should meet you young gentlemen today, and Bolitho Blane thanks you mightily..." He raises the cigarette to his red pouty lips, makes to take a drag, then wanders off across the roof of the school, calling back to us, "Make sure you boys sit a spell before you climb back down!" And since that was the first good advice we'd ever had from a grown-up, we sat there on the roof of our empty high school and watched Bolitho Blane disappear around the southwest corner of the gymnasium like a puff of smoke on a summer breeze.

Paper Shack

Five-thirty a.m. and they are out the basement door and across the dew-covered lawn to the alley leading them to 54th Avenue and on down to the paper shack that sits in a carved recess of the bush at the edge of the city limits. Hal is the super and must unlock the shack for delivery of the day's *Province* newspaper before the ten or twelve paperboys arrive to claim their bundles and complete their routes before breakfast and heading off to school. The Edwin brothers are waiting, hacking a butt and throwing rocks at birds. Joey Scarpazzo pulls in on his Mustang bike, leaning back on his banana seat, spinning low in a skid and shooting gravel against the side of the shack. The padlock pops open and they all pile in, trying to secure a good spot at one of the benches before the place is packed with boys, jostling and sorting their papers, counting copies and stuffing their bags. Violence is never far off and regular spats break out with jabs and flicks of the boots, boyhood tough-guy bravado swirling. "Benchings" are standard fare. "Time for your weekly whipping, Dickie!" and Joey Scarpazzo pushes Dick Swisdale over the centre sorting table, and two other traitors on the other side grab his wrists and hold him there, stretched prone across the bench. Joey rolls one of his canvas sacks into a tight coil, leaving the shoulder strap dangling, the end of his improvised whip. "This is going to hurt you more than it's going to hurt me!" he cackles, then commences to flog Dickie across the thighs and buttocks. After half a dozen lashes, they release him to hoots and hollers, the jostling bodies hefting and shouldering the heavy bags toward the door. "C'mon!" Hal yells. "Get yer sad-sack asses outta here, I wanna go home!" They stumble, bottleneck, and tumble out, two, three bulging bags strung around their necks, or dragged and then precariously balanced on bike carriers and rat traps, moving out like an army convoy into the lightening sky, taking the daily news to the waking world.

Bird Shooting

The butt of the gun stock is braced firmly against his shoulder, the barrel wedged between the inch-wide gap between the door and the door frame. The end of the twelve-gauge Browning Maxus II barrel is levelled at a wooden plaque carving of an eagle, wings spread across the eighteen-inch diameter mounted on the bedroom wall. Bob's arms tremble, sweat beads on his upper lip. "Do it!" someone whispers from behind him. A boom resounds and reverberates off the walls of the hallway, and Bob is down, flat on his ass on the floor, pressed up against the opposite wall. The shotgun stands on end between his splayed legs, an enormous erection. Bob is stunned; the others laugh, point, noticing the red mark above his right eyebrow—a lump now rising—where the barrel kicked up and smacked him. The buckshot has torn through the centre of the plaque and carried on through the wood panelling behind. Bob's dad drives taxi, night shift, and sits at this moment on the Blackstone Hotel stand at Granville and Davie Streets, thinking about duck hunting and wondering when he might next have the chance to get out there.

Shotgun

If only they had not been separated from their friend, they wouldn't be where they are now, which is situated on a small roof over a larger porch outside of and below an upstairs window. They wouldn't be huddled there closely for lack of available space, leaning toward the building for fear of sliding down the angled roof or simply losing balance and somersaulting right off the edge. No, if they had not lost track of their friend, they would have gained access to the house in the usual way—key, lock, door handle, passage—and they would not have needed to prop the ladder against the roof eave and precariously manoeuvre themselves from ladder to roof, to lean, as they do now, against the sloped shingles for balance as they reach for the slightly ajar window of the bedroom that holds the turntable and vinyl records that they are, at this very moment, deliriously intent on listening to. No, they would not be in this situation, they would not be huddling together, unsettlingly unbalanced, facing the long barrel of the Savage 220, twelve-gauge, single-shot break-action shotgun that is now sliding out of the ajar window just above their heads. No, if only they had not lost their friend earlier in the evening, they would not be where they are now.

Umma Gumma

The bedroom is dark, lit only by low-watt red bulbs and the sparkles from a small rotating disco ball. Pink Floyd is being pumped through two Marshall half-stacks and the room is vibrating with the crescendo of "Careful with That Axe, Eugene" when the door bursts open and she is silhouetted, backlit by a sixty-watt bare basement bulb. The spitting image of Bette Davis in *Hush…Hush, Sweet Charlotte* and screaming, "BRETT! BRETT! TURN IT OFF! BRETT! TURN IT OFF!" The three friends are sunk in the couch, too stoned to move or do anything beyond gawk at the visage being seared into their sixteen-year-old minds, but Brett is to his feet and ready to fight. Six-two and looking every bit the twin of Danny the Dealer from *Withnail and I,* he crosses the room in two gigantic steps—"OUT! GET OUT!"—and his mother meekly retreats: "Okay, Brett. Okay…I'm sorry… Okay. Okay." He pokes at her with a broom handle as she slowly climbs the stairs back to the kitchen—*"Get! Get!"*—and then turns back to the sagging jaws, the gaping mouths of his three friends, slamming the door and throwing the carriage bolt—"KEEP THE FUCKING DOOR LOCKED!" And as the adrenaline surge subsides and the music envelops them again, they are truly like "several species of small furry animals gathered together in a cave and grooving with a Pict."

Don't Tell Anyone

Frank was eleven, maybe twelve, when Ron Wolanski, a childhood pal, grabbed him by the wrist and dragged him across the road from the edge of their subdivision and into an open field sparsely populated by building materials for the new housing development that was under construction. Ron was nervous, excited, as he led them over several small berms and across the landscape of sod and mud. When they'd walked for several minutes, Ron stopped and looked Frank right in the eyes and said, "Don't tell anyone." Then he knelt and pulled back the corner of a thick, soiled, canvas tarp. He looked up at Frank, this time with wild eyes. There on the damp, muddy grass was the carcass of a large seagull. Its neck was arced at an odd angle, and on its bright white chest was a splotch of tomato red. Frank noticed how the red of the blood matched perfectly the red of the dot on its bill. He squatted and reached out to touch its soft white plumage. "Where'd it come from? Did you find it?" Ron laughed and gasped out a "Ha!" He stood, and Frank looked up at him. "I shot it," he said, and now he looked more serious, worried, afraid Frank might tell someone. Frank hadn't exhibited the anticipated conspiratorial excitement. "Don't tell anyone, okay? It's against the law to kill a seagull, ya know." He said this with certainty and a bit of a bargaining tone. Frank didn't know how Ron knew this or if it was even true, but he understood all that the words implied. "Don't worry...I won't say anything." Ron crouched back down, flipped the tarp over the bird's blank eye, and got up again. They stood there for a minute not speaking, then turned and headed back toward Ron's house. As they walked, Frank could feel it there between them, the secret, dark and heavy like a storm cloud. Another one—another secret—to be added to the growing list of secrets that were never to be spoken of in adult company: Joe Catelli sold dime bags of weed from his basement bedroom window; Brenda McAllister had been taken into the woods by an old man and made to do things; Liam Storm's older brother had a pound of hash; Alex Crawford had sex with his sister… It went on and on. He tried to forget about them, but they stuck and surfaced at the oddest times: in the bath, walking to school in the rain, hands stuffed in his pockets. And they felt like that—the secrets—like his hands, deep in dark pockets.

Two

SEISMIC SHIFTS

The Work of the Devil

The rash had been there, off and on, for a couple of years. It seemed to flare up in summer so was perhaps just a heat rash, though his doctor had never confirmed or denied this diagnosis. Instead, the doctor prescribed a lotion—one that appeared to be comprised, largely, of water and menthol oil—and advised him on the twice-daily application. When he asked the doctor if the rash could be caused by sitting in his leather office chair for extended periods, he got no reply, except a reiteration from the doctor to use the lotion twice a day, and the prognosis that the rash should clear up in no time. While pulling his pants back on, he asked the doctor, whose back was now to him, what he thought of the idea that rashes, carbuncles, boils, and such were the work of the Devil. He couldn't tell if the doctor's shoulders actually lurched up and down (as with a shrug or, maybe, a chuckle), and he certainly couldn't know if the doctor had rolled his eyes or not, the doctor's white back being all he could see. In his head he thought he heard the doctor—or some voice—say, *Well, we can't discount the possibility of anything, now can we?* He sat up a little straighter, a little taller at this moment, and said, "What?" "Let's see you again in a few weeks," the doctor said, and handed him a prescription for the menthol-infused lotion.

The Dental Hygienist

It was and wasn't what he thought the job would be. It was mostly dealing with teeth, but he always imagined his day would be parcelled up more, broken into periods of cleaning and scraping, checking the depths of pockets, flossing and polishing teeth that would never get any whiter, regardless of how much attention he paid them. But he also thought that significant portions of his days would be consumed by other, related duties: taking X-rays, prepping moulds for crowns, overlays, and caps, and sending these off for orthodontic construction. But this wasn't the case. No, most of his days were spent with his fingers in the mouths of other people. Scraping—both ultrasonically and manually—polishing, and suctioning the saliva and rinse that always accumulated much more quickly than he expected, resulting in excess fluids escaping in a flow down the patient's cheek and neck, requiring quick and gentle dabbing with paper napkins. Sometimes, when working far back in the mouth, on the molars, he would pinch a lip between a tooth and the edge of his hand. Sometimes he would notice this—see the patient flinch—and not release the pressure until the patient waved or made some unintelligible sound. And then he would say, "Sorry," and carry on as if nothing had happened. But, of course, something had happened, and both he and the patient knew that something had happened. At times like these he would often hum softly while renewing his work. This seemed to comfort them.

The Proselytizers

Marty McTigue had come down to the coast from the Okanagan with no distinct plan, no contacts, and very little money. His goal was to live in Vancouver, a city by the sea. Where he lived in the Okanagan it was dry, almost desert-like, and he had always pined for a place near the water—the ocean—where he could hear waves lapping at the shore and seagulls crying in the air. His father had died exactly one month prior to the day he boarded his bus for the coast. It would take six or seven days to get there if he walked, but the bus would have him in Vancouver in five hours. He always marvelled at this fact and had the greatest respect for the pioneers who had traversed the mountains, valleys, and rivers by horse, canoe, and foot on their trek to the coast. After the death of his father—a bad ladder fall in the orchard—his mother had decided to sell the farm and move to Vernon to be closer to her sister, who had moved there with her husband, who had taken up the trade of cheese making. Marty had taken this as a sign, perhaps from God, that it was time to make his break. Vernon was the wrong direction, had no sea, and he had no interest in learning the intricacies of cheese production. The bus fare was $39 one way and his mother paid for the ticket and gave him another $500 to, as she said, tide him over until he got on his feet. The first person he met in Vancouver was a young gentleman by the name of Arnold, the same name his father had been given, and he took this as another sign. Arnold was well-dressed, in a pressed white shirt, tie, and black slacks. He was giving away a magazine called *Awake!* in the waiting area of the bus station on Terminal Avenue. Marty asked Arnold if he, too, might find such a job, and Arnold said there was always room in their family, and within twenty-four hours he had a fine, pressed white shirt, a tie, and a pair of new black slacks. And he got to work with Arnold as a team, day in and day out. They often spent hours on the streets near the beach or other areas of the waterfront, where the sea was never far from sight.

Fuun

It was fairly normal lunch-hour antics: teens smoking, talking bravado, blowing smoke rings to the ceiling, grabbing food, throwing food, stuffing some of that food into laughing extended mouths, and stretching gum from lip-glossed lips. There was nothing extraordinary about this lunch break, nothing unusual about the frenzied, overlapping, half-finished, rapid-fire sentences, the electric energy in the room. Until the explosion occurred. Then the silence, a peculiar silence. Then the urging calls. The *Holy fuck!*s, the *Oh my god!*s and then the frenetic energy that rushed back in to fill the vacuum. The explosion had been the discharge of a single-barrel twelve-gauge shotgun, combined with the destruction of the bathroom door that the propelling buckshot had caused. The hallway filled with smoke and gunpowder stink. Then came the moaning and whimpering. Two teens were in the bathroom, behind what was left of the hollow bathroom door. Brad stood two feet back, the shotgun still hanging from his slack arms. Inside the bathroom, behind the splintered door, Ken Neufeld leaned against the wall, holding his side that had caught the outer edge of the buckshot's spray. On the floor at his feet was Tak Sakamura, moaning and oozing out a large wet patch of his midsection. It was clear that he was bleeding to death, and already the kids filling the hall, trying to look over shoulders, were thinking about Tak's older brother, Tashi, an intense guy, a black belt in karate, and a known scrapper. They were also thinking about how they were glad that they weren't Brad.

Blasting Caps

As soon as the cop walked into the classroom and held up the small specimen between his thumb and index finger, Richard "Dickie" Swisdale knew exactly what was going to be said. "This," said the officer, "is a blasting cap." *Yes,* thought Dickie. "And even though they are very small, they can be quite dangerous," the constable continued. "If you see one, do not handle it. You could lose a finger, or an eye. Contact one of your teachers, or a parent." He went on to tell the class that several of these had gone missing from a nearby construction site and the authorities didn't want anyone to be unnecessarily harmed. What the officer did not tell them, and probably didn't want anyone to know at this point, was that there were also two sticks of dynamite and a plunger missing from the same construction site, and Dickie Swisdale knew who had them and where they were hidden at this very moment. Delmore Dodson had snapped the hasp lock with a crowbar and helped himself to the blasting caps, the dynamite, and a few other engineering supplies from the city workers' trailer. The blasting caps were being rigged into a makeshift pipe bomb. The dynamite would be saved for a more impressive display, like, perhaps, blowing out one side of the retaining wall of the pit at the city dump. The cop thanked the class for their attention and informed them that "several suspects" were currently under observation and the police were confident they would soon retrieve the missing explosives. Dickie Swisdale sat erect, near the back of the class, and had to work hard to not turn around to see the eyes he could feel boring into the back of his head.

The Flying "A"

The Austin Flying "A" swerved sharply from side to side, veered back and forth before its left-front tire caught the median in the middle of the road, flipping the car to its roof and sending it on a twenty-foot slide, ending its topsy-turvy trajectory at the entrance to the McDonald's drive-through at the intersection of Broadway and Boundary Road. He found himself on all fours in a foreign world of synthetic fabric, padded foam, curves that belied the flat-surface world he had come to expect...and glass—small cubes of thick glass...and two shapes over his shoulder, hanging like inverted gravestones...and voices, voices... He crawls around in a circle on this spongy ground—*What is it? Where am I?* Then an opening, and he moves, like exiting a burrow. He stands and his world resurrects. The Flying "A" is upside down on its now crumpled roof, oil streaming down the front panels. Ronnie, who had been driving, is holding his right arm, supporting it at the elbow as blood trails from his hand down his arm. A skinny, wide-eyed MacDonald's employee in a paper "Trainer" cap and holding a Hamburg broom says, "Wow! Should I call the cops?" Before the cops can arrive, the boys have rocked, rolled, and righted the Austin A30, climbed in, and managed to lurch away into the oncoming traffic lane, stuck in third gear, around the end of the median, and off up the incline of Boundary Road, due south to the corner of the city they call "Home."

Tumble

There was an audible *click*, then the right rear door was open and he was gone. They'd taken the corner fast and it was a hairpin, so it wasn't entirely surprising that the door had popped open on this old car, but, nonetheless, it was still a surprise. And because of their speed they were a fair ways up the road by the time the Hillman Minx came to a stop and they could turn to look back through the oval rear window and rear-view mirror to see Spats slowly getting to his feet, dusting off his denim overalls, slapping his hands together to free his palms of dirt and gravel. Then they had to laugh—the other four, safe in their seats and companionship—laugh hard and long, Mouse saying, "He was there and then he was gone! A *click* and he was gone!" The Hillman idled loudly for a few moments and then they heard footsteps on gravel, and Spats tucked his head into the car and reclaimed his seat in the rear-right corner, slamming the door, perhaps a bit harder than necessary, flipping his long blond shag-cut hair from the collar of his jean jacket, and then laughing hard and loud, a real belly laugh, and the others laughed again too, as if they hadn't laughed yet. And they all realized, however subconsciously, that there was a *click* of some sort waiting for them all. A *click* and then they too would just be gone. Then the Hillman pulled away and began its slow climb from the waterfront toward the Marine Building and the heart of the city, and, for the moment, all was well.

Funny Odd

He was naked except for a pair of brown socks. He walked, as people are fond of saying, with purpose. His arms swung jauntily, his stride strong and steady. He held his head straight and erect as he headed north down the hill toward False Creek. Arnie and Bob were driving west on Broadway and approaching the intersection at Ash when the naked man approached Broadway and proceeded to cross, arms swinging, moving with what appeared to be purpose, hell-bent, as some would say, on his destination. Arnie looked over at Bob, exhaling a blast of cigarette smoke into the interior of the Volkswagen van, and laughed hard—"Ha! Ha! Ha!" And he laughed, some might say, because it was funny—odd funny—to see a man walking, with great purpose, down a city street, wearing absolutely nothing but a pair of brown socks.

Opera Man

For years he strolled Broadway, from Main Street to Granville, openly singing opera—do you actually sing opera or is there a fancy word for that bizarre style of vocalization? His singing—and his manner of exhibitionism—was not the kind that made the viewer withdraw or made one want to give the person in question a wide berth as they passed. People approaching were not prompted to cross the street out of nervous uncertainty. No, Opera Man, as he came to be known, instilled a sense of Old World warmth, much like a group of carollers do, hearkening one back to an imagined time when humans gathered outdoors, in the common green, and entertained one another over a warm mug of mead or mulled wine. And he would walk in a slow, easy gait, his bearded chin of childish curls tilting to the sky, arias of Puccini or Mozart or Rossini echoing off the concrete foyers of the medical building and the many hotels along his route. And then he was gone, a fixture suddenly no longer seen, heard, felt. As if, perhaps, he had died or moved to another city or country or had, one day, for reasons known to no one but himself, decided to "sing no more." Or maybe there was no conscious decision in it; maybe the song had simply ceased. And then a decade, maybe twelve years, had passed, and in a coffee shop on Broadway a stranger in conversation at the next table says, "Have you ever seen the guy that—" "Yes!"

Cuffed, in Car

He slapped him across the face, the slovenly attired cop did. Not an open-handed forceful slap, but a casual back-hander, after which he took a long drag on his cigarette and said, "Shut your mouth and face forward." The boy was only sixteen and couldn't do anything to defend himself as his hands were cuffed behind his back. He was also drunk and a little high from smoking pot or hash or whatever they had been up to that summer night. He couldn't quite remember how he'd ended up with his face crammed up against the back-seat window of the squad car, straining to keep his balance every time the car took a corner or sped away from a stoplight. And the slap hadn't hurt. What bothered him about it was the flagrant abuse of power exhibited by the two pigs who were transporting him to the city lock-up. And now he remembered how this had started. He'd been hiding out down a short flight of stairs at the back of the church when, suddenly, he'd been dragged by his hair backwards up the steps. His friends were gone and there was just him and the cop, moving toward the open back door of the squad car. He heard the word *punk* and then his face was scraping along the synthetic and plastic fibres that made up the upholstery of the car's back seat. This was before the slap in the face and the sagely advice from the senior officer and just prior to him shooting his mouth off about power freaks and their fine display of enforcing the Queen's Law and just before the junior officer in the driver's seat exploded in an embarrassing show of rage as he twisted his body toward the back seat and, with a spitting, contorted face, screamed, "Shut up! Shut up! Shut your fucking mouth! You have no idea how fucking lucky you are!" That made him wonder about his friends, and he wondered if maybe they were somewhere down an alley getting punched and kicked, or behind the church getting slapped around in the back of the paddy wagon. Was he lucky? And for the first time he realized that they might not be driving him to the lock-up but maybe to an isolated part of town for a two-on-one display of fine Canadian non-tribunal justice. Would he then still be considered "lucky"?

Horse Tranqs

Upon getting in the car, they had taken two capsules each. They were heading "up-country," as people liked to say. Approximately five hours on the highway. Well, four actually. The first hour would be spent just getting out of the city. Two each of the large white-and-red capsules containing the drug. The idea was that they'd be good and stoned by the time they got there, by the time they pulled into the campsite and met up with the others. The traffic funnelled up 12th Avenue to Grandview Highway and on toward the entrance to the Trans-Canada Highway. They had procured the drugs from an acquaintance who went by the nickname of "The Pharaoh"—that's what people called him, because of how his hair tumbled down in tight kinks in the shape of a pyramid. Someone said, "Here comes the Pharaoh," and it stuck. The Pharaoh had handed them a small baggie of ten capsules, grinned, and said, "It's good shit." Forty-five minutes into the journey, the one in the navigator's seat said, "I'm not feeling a thing." "Neither am I," said the one at the wheel. "We should have taken them on an empty stomach." They travelled like this, uttering the occasional vague comment, staring out at the passing trees, the mountainsides that looked like they might tumble down at any moment, the rivers that resembled slow-flowing mercury. The navigator lowered the map like a veil across his knees, said they had to watch for Junction 15, and leaned in to turn up the volume of the music, only to discover that the car stereo was not on. The driver grinned and, with his eyes solidly on the road, said, "Good shit."

Camel Saddle

Kent Burbidge had a brother four or five years his senior. This older brother and a friend had travelled to Afghanistan long before North Americans spoke casually of this landlocked country in Central-South Asia. The plan was to spend a few days in Kabul, then head north to Balkh Province and Mazar-i-Sharif to visit the famous Blue Mosque, before heading into the mountains in search of a trustworthy supplier of locally manufactured hashish. But events did not unfold exactly as envisioned. Such as having their heads shaved as a condition of entry at a checkpoint outside Herat. *Why must they shave off their hippie hair?* "Because," a smiling guard said, "you want to pass, no?" Their entree into the heart of Afghan hash production involved a byzantine series of meetings and introductions. They got cold stares that asked: *Who are these guys? Maybe CIA?* Eventually, in Nakhonay, Kandahar Province, where some thirty-six years later Sapper Brian Collier of 1 Combat Engineer Regiment, CFB Edmonton, would be killed by an IED, they managed to procure a pound of hand-pressed hashish (the highly cherished black "charas," its soft, fudge-like texture a favourite among connoisseurs). They wrapped the hashish tight in cheesecloth, then bound it in several layers of duct tape, before inserting the package into the lining of a camel saddle bought in Kandahar's Shahi Bazaar market for twenty-five U.S. dollars, which they then mailed "Post Express" to a friend back in Vancouver, Canada. Upon their return some twenty-eight days later, they could not get on the phone—the landline—fast enough, dialling the number of their friend, Ty Stone, getting him on the phone, and then, with high-strung, kinetic energy, asking: "Did you get the parcel we sent?" Ty was excited to hear

Rick's voice, his friend safely back from faraway foreign lands. "You guys are back?" Rick was getting impatient, desperate to know if Ty had the camel saddle sitting on a shelf in his bedroom. "Yes, yes! We're back! Did you get the parcel?" Ty was confused. "Parcel?" "Yes!" Rick said. "We sent you a gift from Afghanistan...about a month ago. You didn't get it? Are you sure?" "Whaddya mean?" "Awww, shit!" Rick yelled, slamming the ebony handset into the cradle of the Bakelite telephone. Ty stood in the afternoon summer light of the kitchen in his parents' three-bedroom Mid-Century Builder on Battison Street in southeast Vancouver, lemon-yellow walls and white lace curtains adorned with small red strawberries, holding the dead phone line, feeling dejected and hurt by his two friends he hadn't seen all summer. "Yeah, nice talking to you too," he said before returning the matching lemon-yellow handset to its wall-mounted cradle. Rick Burbidge punched a hole in his bedroom wall and spat out the word "Fuck!" a dozen times before settling on the edge of his bed, rubbing his fingers through his inch-long hair. They had planned and executed everything so carefully. Exactly ten days later another call was placed between the two residences, this time initiated by Ty Stone, ringing the landline of Richard Burbidge, seven blocks away. Amazingly, Rick was home and not shipping out on his father's seiner off the shore of Ucluelet on Vancouver Island's west coast, to work out the remainder of the summer making money and getting seasick. He picked up the receiver of the loud-ringing ebony phone and uttered the common greeting of the day: "Hello?" Ty was excited: "It's here! Your package. It arrived!" Rick fell back against the tiled kitchen counter. "I'll be right over!" he said. "Don't. Go. Anywhere!" He slammed down the phone before grabbing his jean jacket and heading out the door.

Hot Knifing

The smoke billows up, thick and grey, like a miniature volcano, and into the open end of the toilet-paper roll. The soft, black Afghany hashish smoulders quickly and easily when compressed between the two glowing red ends of the heated butter knives. The delivery system is efficient and fast. Explosive ignition, one deep inhale, and the lungs receive an abrupt assault of torched cannabis resin, instantly delivering the THC to the bloodstream, the brain, the senses. *Heat. Press. Inhale. Repeat.* Time slows. Sound muffles. Someone is coughing—both distant and close at the same time. There is a knock at the door.

Pipe Bomb

Doug Colchester was fascinated by explosives. He somehow gained possession of gunpowder, blasting caps, and even once had in his hold two sticks of dynamite. Today he was removing the powder from a box of 30-06 shells, amassing it to be combined with a handful of ball bearings in a length of one-inch-diameter copper pipe. Bent at a forty-five-degree angle, one end was crimped to form a makeshift handle, the other half was the "barrel" to be filled; a fuse devised from a full pack of firecracker fuses, twined together like a Lilliputian's rope, ran the length of the barrel. Doug gently packed the powder and projectiles as Dickie Swisdale watched, sucking on a Labatt 50 stubby. "You'll blow yer fuckn hand off ya light that!" said Dickie. Doug snickered like a lunatic at his workbench, tightening the vice a half-crank, sealing the end of the handle. This, his theory went, would assure the explosion would be forced out the barrel end. Eleven-thirty p.m. was the chosen test time and behind the community centre was the chosen test site. Three or four of them stood behind Doug as he held out his right arm straight and rigid. The fuse dangled from the barrel end, and Dickie squatted down and flicked his BIC. Orange sparks jumped and climbed the rope as the others backed away. The boom was deafening. Smoke floated around them. The fire flash at the bottom of the poorly sealed handle was the last thing they saw. As the smoke cleared, they moved forward to inspect the buckshot pattern the ball bearings had made in the wall of the community centre. Their fingers ran over the edges of the splintered wood. Doug stood there holding his burnt hand in his good one. "It worked! It worked!" he kept saying. They continued to run their fingers over the splintered wood of the violated wall. And then, as sirens grew closer, they ran too.

The Waltz

The screen door bursts open from the weight of their bodies, hits the porch railing, and bounces back against them as they stumble out in a tight embrace, shirts being pulled, bunched in tightened fists, punches being thrown. Though Darrel is only sixteen, he stands at six-one and is now face to face with his father as the old man swings another awkward punch. They spin, like dancers, hit the rail, and almost trip down the tall flight of stairs. Darrel's three friends stand in the alley at the backyard gate, stunned by what they are witnessing. They've never seen anything like this. As if on a small stage, two adversaries fighting it out. But here was father and son, locked in bare-fisted battle, intent on killing any love that was left.

Destination: Rez

Dickie is sitting on the cab stand outside the Cozy Corner grocery at the intersection of Hastings and Abbott Streets in Vancouver's Downtown Eastside, directly across from the Sunrise Hotel. He's nineteen and trying to make some extra cash to help him get through college, but the courses, and the working at night, are killing him. He's only been driving hack for six months and still hasn't got a handle on it, hasn't learned how to work the system—grabbing flags and other unreported fares—how to hustle and move and make a decent buck. He is checking his trip sheet when the passenger-side doors swing open and five young guys pile in—three in the back, two in the front, violating the rules of transport that stress that a carrier may only convey a maximum of four passengers at any one time. The guy closest to him says, "Capilano Reserve!" as the two doors slam. Dickie tries to explain that he can't take five passengers, and they all hoot and laugh and say, "Let's go!" Dickie reluctantly swings the cab out into traffic and starts to head east toward Hastings Park and the Second Narrows Bridge as the guy who is squeezed into the middle of the seat beside him grabs his trip-sheet clipboard, shouting—"Hey, he's got a hundred and fifty bucks logged!" The others laugh, and the guy tosses the clipboard onto the dash as they zoom past the Astoria Hotel, where two guys are engaged in a tear-down exchange of differing opinions. A tuck down Clark Drive and soon they are turning onto Powell Street and heading for Nanaimo. Dickie hears a beer can pop and one of the three in the back barks "YEE-HAW!" and as he feels his back tighten up, he starts to worry—if someone barfs in the cab he'll get dinged seventy-five bucks for clean-up. They sail down the slope behind Hastings Park racetrack, past the horse stables and New Brighton Park and the outdoor pool where Dickie and his friends often go in the summer to smoke a joint, drink a few concealed beers, and read a book on a towel in the sun. Last year it was *Big Sur,* Kerouac's ninth novel, detailing his descent into alcoholism and delirium tremens. Scared Dickie straight for a few weeks. "Driver! You wanna beer?" comes from behind him. "Thanks, but not while I'm driving." "Ah, fuck that! Have a beer!" A can of Labatt Blue sails over his shoulder, hits the dashboard, then bounces off his knee before dropping to the floor mat. Hoots erupt and two guys in the back seat yell "Cheers!" and Dickie hears the soft clicking of tin cans, followed by belches. He worries that he will have to eat this fare, that they will stiff him for the trip, and he'll have to deadhead it back into the city. Wasted time, lost money. Then the cab is sailing up onto the bridge, and his mind goes to the collapse that happened during construction, a calculation error by a young engineer. But what does it matter, really. Several section spans fell, and eighteen workers died, and one of those who had died on that day in June 1958, at three-forty in the afternoon, was the father of a grade-school friend, Leena Popovitch, and that is who he thinks of now as they zoom across the span toward the North Shore Mountains and the land named in honour of Indigenous Chief Joe Capilano. Somewhere along the Dollarton Highway, one of them says, "Pull over here," and Dickie swings the cab onto the gravel shoulder and stops. The five guys pile out and one of them turns, says, "Thanks, man," and tosses two twenties onto the front seat. "Keep the change, eh." Dickie looks down at the bills, sees that someone has turned the Queen into a pirate, giving her an eye patch and moustache with a ballpoint pen. Dickie laughs and toots the horn, and the guys turn and raise their beers as he pulls away.

Viaduct 360

The car was spinning in a complete 360 rotation on the snow-slicked surface of the Georgia Street viaduct. At about the 280-degree point of the dreamy, floating roundabout, a small flock of seagulls arced up and over the railing, soared past them on a sharp seventeen-degree angle, gliding in perfect formation across the movie screen of the car's windshield, wings white and stark against the black sky. They—the two occupants of the out-of-control car—completed their silent rotation and resumed travelling east, past the obnoxious neon art installation—"EVERYTHING IS GOING TO BE ALRIGHT"—that loomed high above the core of the Downtown Eastside, and on toward the Main Street exit. "Holy shit," said the one in the passenger seat. Not in astonishment, the driver was certain, that they had completed their stunt-driving antics unscathed on the overpass at one-thirty in the morning but by the surprising behaviour of the gulls, which, it is well-known, do not *usually* fly at night.

Large Pizza

He is driving, one eye on the traffic ahead of him and the other on the large pizza box on the passenger seat beside him. His right hand is trying to pop the staple holding the lid closed while his right foot hops from brake pedal to gas as the mid-evening traffic ebbs out of the city. He just manages to get the lid open as a driver three or four cars ahead hits the brakes, sending up a blast of red alert warning, and the cars behind follow suit, seriously abbreviating their travel on the avenue, and luckily his foot is mid-hover over the brake when his road eye signals the brain, and his foot stomps the brake pedal the way you might stomp a bug, radically disturbing the pizza's inertia, sending it forward and up, lid open in a spectacular display of topsy-turvy motion, coming to rest face down on the debris-laden floor mat. At the curb, the car idles in its design, and he does his best to not think of the food item as "completely ruined" but only as "altered" while he works to right the situation, individual slices succumbing to gravity or clinging to their neighbour. And when he finally raises a wedge to his mouth, it is a wonderful, delicious pizza that enters his sense cavern, his tongue exploding with the tang of tomato sauce, the rich creaminess of melted cheese, the spicy grease accent of cured meat, all in all an extremely comforting effect, and, say what you will, marred only slightly by the occasional crunch of gravel.

Sky-Watcher

He would most often see her near the Hudson's Bay store, on the Georgia Street side, in downtown Vancouver. She appeared to be locked in a state of semi-paralysis, her arms seized across her midsection, hands gripping opposite elbows, torso erect, and her head—the most distinguishing feature of her riveting image—arced at a fifteen-degree angle, chin pointing to the sky, hair hanging like an enormous clump of matted wool, or a bee swarm from the branch of a tree. And it was this, this unfathomable snarl of human hair, that seemed to be her terrible weight, the inescapable burden that yarded her head on its horrible axis. She was locked in a skyward gaze—searching, waiting, and in her short, measured steps she exercised caution, slowly shuffling her rigid being along the downtown street, as if half-expecting a punishing bolt to strike down from the heavens through her self-imposed position as Lady Oracle of Terminal City, devastating the populace that milled around her. She moved with the patience of a phantom. And her dress—always the same—was made of a washed-out floral pattern from another era, something a great-aunt or grandmother might have worn on laundry day or while canning fruit in the still heat of summer. Thin, worn, as if she had wandered in from the orchard and just never made it back.

Rosary

For years he was a fixture at the intersection of Granville and Georgia Streets, at the northwest corner of the Bay, under the street-cover overhang. Immobile, frozen in place, staring out across the intersection. His gaunt frame draped in a worn, plain brown suit that had the glossy sheen of fabric having been folded and stored but rarely laundered. His face and neck were marred by scabby splotches that made one think of poverty, malnutrition, deep worry. His gaze never wavered as he stood there, leaning slightly forward, arm extended, hand holding a small wooden cross from which dangled a beaded rosary about twelve to sixteen inches long. It looked old or Old World. And from his anchored spot, where a steady stream of shoppers and office workers passed, he made no effort to engage or proselytize, but seemed simply to be on a mission of "bearing witness," and he had done so daily since February 24, 1972, when, in his small rooming-house room on Homer Street, the Lord had spoken to him from a chest of drawers, telling him that there was much work to be done, and that that work and devoted toil must commence immediately.

The Balcony

Royston Fellers awoke, awkward, discomfited, bent-backed over a fourteen-inch granite gardening stone on the floor of an unfurnished eighteen-storey apartment building in Vancouver's West End. A bleary-eyed, dry-mouthed, thump-pulsed specimen of teenage all-night debauchery, he attempted to raise his head as Bellestar Ptomac burst out of the washroom swinging a distended condom, a sunglow egg yolk straining at the nipple cup with every enthusiastic twirl. "We had you sucking on this last night!" she whooped. Royston managed to prop himself up on an elbow and was about to attempt basic verbalization—a "Good morning" or "Holy shit, am I wrecked"—when Manzies Beauregard waltzed like an Egyptian from the bedroom toward the kitchen, and from his vantage point on the wall-to-wall olefin Berber carpet, Royston could see into the small washroom where *MANSON KILLERS!* was scrawled across the mirror in poinsettia-red lipstick. Pania Difalco emerged from the kitchen nook in a Jesus bathrobe, hoisting a glass of Prosecco in a *cheers!*, pronouncing, "Where's Keedy? Where's my boy!" whilst looking out over his flute of fizzling wine, past Royston in his stone-quarry bed, to the balcony window with its southerly vantage of downtown, and the Fairview Slopes beyond, only to proclaim: "Oh, there he is!" Royston rolled his head on his stone pillow and gazed the length of his own body to see Keedy—yes, it was Keedy—hanging by his fingertips from the eighteenth-floor balcony railing. Smirking, he called out, "Royston, look at me! Look at me, Roy!" Bellestar spun on her six-inch stiletto heels and twirled the condom yo-yo again: "Did you hear me? We had you sucking on this in your sleep!" And she said it like it was the funniest thing anyone had ever said.

Boats in a Boxcar

It's 110 degrees inside the railcar. Mid-August and the air is thick, even at 10:30 a.m. The car is packed ceiling to floor with aluminum car-top boats, banded together at bow and stern with fourteen-gauge baling wire. Sykes and three others move in slow and squeeze between the stacks, sucking stomachs in, rubbing the oily dust on the backs of their jeans and T-shirts. Pulling at the gunwales, turning legs sideways to get a purchase on the edge of the lower boat, hoisting slowly, gently, they move their bodies up toward the ceiling and into the thick hot air. Knees knock, elbows bonk, making hollow kettle-drum sounds to the accompaniment of "Fuck!" "Shit!" Careful. Steady. Balance. Pull the tin snips from back pockets—*Don't drop them!* Wedge and twist the snip blade under the one-inch tightly cinched high-tensile steel-band strapping. Squeeze the hands, grips together, and when they go, when the shears cut a diagonal slice, it is a *BONG!* Like a huge guitar string snapping. The stack of boats jump an inch, spring with the power released—now tighter in the car, even less room between the roof and their work world. Now focus on the baling wire—hard, thick as string licorice—wiggle, work the cutters back and forth, sweat and dust coating their exposed skin. Squeeze and twist and squeeze more, and finally—*parrrong!*—the wire gives, the interstacked, interlocked, eight-, ten-, twelve-foot car-toppers spring free, and the wrestling, lifting, tilting, wrangling begins. Out of their slots and lowering them toward the open sliding door of the boxcar. "HOW THE FUCK DO THEY GET THEM IN HERE!" echoes through the car. The squeezing, snapping, cutting, pulling, tilting, and lowering carries on through the day until the last silver boat is dragged toward the door—

their hands and arms too sore to grip or lift. "Fuck me," one of them says. And behind them, graffitied on the back wall of the boxcar in huge red letters:

HEY VANCOUVER!!!
—Jerry + Dan, Dayton, Ohio

Patats Floor

They were the best of friends. They had worked together for years, through many seasons of inclement weather. And as their friendship had inevitably grown deeper, they tended to drink together—socially at first, and then more seriously, competitively, later. And so it was not odd when, at the end of a long evening of drinking—that involved, for one of them, vomiting in a host's closet (mistaking a clothes hamper for a toilet), and for the other, a headlong plunge down a flight of frost-covered stairs (after bidding the host a jaunty "Good night!")—that their focus would turn to thoughts of food. No, it was not uncommon for them, in such situations, to turn their attention to food and, upon arriving—somehow—at the basement apartment of the one, for the other to offer to make them some home-cut hash browns and eggs, for the one liked to cook and was very adept at pulling hearty dishes together at a moment's notice. And the hash browns, with onions, peppers, and sausage—more of a "hash" than hash browns—tumbled, in a drunken twist of the wrist, cast-iron pan and all, to land face down on the linoleum floor. They laughed, ate them anyway, and, as good friends do, raised their mugs of beer and toasted their latest creation—"Patats Floor!"

Distractions

He had written a lot of books, more books than any one person needed to write. Mid-mornings he liked to take a break from his writing routine and go for coffee at his favourite diner. This routine quickly became common knowledge among the literati, and soon enough many younger, aspiring writers would show up at the senior writer's local diner to also have coffee and, hopefully, be regaled by the senior writer. He would entertain them with his many stories of success, failure, run-ins and fights with editors and publishers over the years, debates with colleagues, and other anecdotal tales accumulated over his decades-long career and through the writing and publishing of his one-hundred-plus books. Between the tall tales, someone would always pop a coin into the tiny jukebox in the booth, because such automated music-playing devices were so rare these days, and it was nostalgic to play some of those old songs by bands like the Troggs, Martha and the Vandellas, or the Strawberry Alarm Clock. On occasion, one of the junior writers would feel slightly embarrassed by their song selection, but once the senior writer began regaling them again, the laughs would start and the embarrassment would soon be forgotten.

Red Flag

The doctor turns toward Frank, needle in hand, poised upright, and says, "Okay, try not to move." He is stunned by the situation, the rapid-fire progression from "Take a seat," to a quick spread of the eyelids, an "Uh-huh," a turning away, and now the doctor is back above him and leaning in with a large syringe, saying, "Try not to move." The nurse puts a gentle hand on his shoulder, says, "Try holding your breath." He does, and as the tip of the needle nears his eyeball, he freezes—not breathing, not moving as the needle goes in, into the corner of his eye. *How far? Where does it go?* He can feel his eye getting cold, the side of his head going numb. Then the needle slides out, cool and smooth. A clamp is put in place to hold his lids apart, and then the eye surgeon leans in again with what Frank can only assume is a scalpel. "You'll feel a little tugging, maybe hear a little scraping." He feels and hears: tugging, scraping, like sand being scraped out of the corner of a jacket pocket. The nurse runs a rill of thick warm fluid into his eye as the doc says, "That oughta do it," then dabs his cheek with a cotton swab and gently presses a soft pad to his eye, saying, "Hold that there for fifteen minutes." He stumbles back onto the street, Kingsway near Metrotown, and passes people hurrying along the sidewalk. The SkyTrain swooshes by. Frank hasn't been out this way in years, and out of his one good eye he can see that the area is now populated by Vietnamese and sushi restaurants. He stumbles along in the afternoon sunshine for a block or two before slowly peeling away the cotton pad from his eye. Looking down, he can't help but think that what he sees is a very good facsimile of the Japanese national flag.

Numerology

The digital numbers on his iPhone display had been freaking him out. Well, not the actual numbers, but their combinations. For weeks he had been noticing unusual—what he previously would have thought of as "coincidental"—combinations that were starting to feel like more than coincidence—9:11, 3:45, 6:16, 4:44—and it was starting to get to him. Like Rosencrantz, who incessantly flips a coin, disbelieving each time that it will again be heads. He presses the button on his phone and is met with symmetry, anagrams, and disquieting "order"—9:19, 5:43, 10:10. What were the chances? What would Wittgenstein say? Did it mean anything more than the time of day? Could it be someone from the great beyond trying to make contact? The doubters always say that if there were an afterlife, the dead would surely make contact. Well? Maybe they're trying. Maybe the problem is us. We are the ones failing to see the signs. But what if? How to send messages back? He depresses the power button again—5:25—and is no longer surprised by what he sees. Maybe it is enough to acknowledge the contact. Simply let them know they are heard.

The Hoarder

The suite inspection would take only five to ten minutes, once they got in. The inspection had to be conducted by two members of the Inspection Committee, for potential, future "legal" reasons. Lorna opened the door slowly, just two inches, and peered out. Her large, tinted sunglasses covered most of her upper face, and a floral bandana swathed her head, pulled low to her eyebrows. A small gold sliding chain lock was on the door, so it closed softly for a moment while the chain slid in its track and then the door opened again. Harris had warned Casey beforehand—no, *warned* is perhaps too strong a word; *cautioned* might be better, but no, there wasn't any real danger. So *cautioned* is probably a bit hyperbolic; *advised* is more accurate. Yes, advised. He was under *advisement*. Lorna whispered, "Hello," and Casey and Harris stepped into the hallway, clipboards and pens in hand. Lorna moved deep into the living room, and Casey and Harris lingered near the door, adjusting to the tight confines created by the stacks of magazines, newspapers, and boxes that rose floor to ceiling along every available wall. The carpeted pathway that Lorna had trod was about twelve to fourteen inches wide and they, too, followed it toward the living room. It was near impossible to "inspect" the condition of the walls or the floor, as they were hidden behind the teetering paper archives. The inspectors ticked the tiny boxes on their inspection sheets and roamed slowly from room to room, glancing at the walls and ceilings, commenting that paint here or there could possibly be done in the next year or two. Lorna's head was tilted down so they couldn't really see her eyes behind the rose-tinted sunglasses. She seemed to be humming a soft tune. Harris and Casey moved toward the door to the hallway, thanked Lorna for allowing them to inspect the suite, and stepped out into the hall. And as Casey bent to pick up his dropped pen, he was certain he heard the chain of the door lock slide softly in its channel.

The Ride

Frank Amubian and his nordic pal Mikhail Jensen were in Gastown, underage and trying to get served. Some of the divey joints cared as little about your legal age as they did about your general well-being. They *did* get served and they *did* drink. Maybe it was the Anchor, or the Grand Union, maybe the Dodson. In some of these low-track bars, if you kept your eyes down, stared at the red tablecloth, the beers would just drop. And after several rounds, and pizza after, they were back on Main Street, the #3 heading south. Off at Kingsway, their thumbs went out… It was late and they had no idea if another bus was coming or not. Two guys didn't have the easiest time landing a ride, so they would walk awhile, then try again. As they approached the Biltmore Hotel, a dark green sedan pulled over. A two-door, and the passenger hopped out, pulled the seat forward, said, "Get in!" And, after exchanging glances of "Okay?" they got in and slumped into the sagging seats, taking in the aroma of old vinyl and the pine-tree air freshener that dangled from the rear-view mirror, swinging in spirals as the driver screeched away. They raced up the curb lane, then cut in front of traffic and accelerated through the S-curve toward Fraser. "You guys wanna come over for a beer?" was hollered out over the roar of the 283 Chevy engine and the strains of Deep Purple's "Highway Star." Frank was drumming his hands on his knees and looked over at Mikhail, who shrugged his shoulders and said, "Sure, why not!" The car took a sharp right at Norquay Park, across from Wally's Burgers, drifted about a half block, then pulled onto the gravel shoulder to park. They were deep in working-class East Van now, and the houses were nothing special. Around back of a two-bedroom stucco bungalow, and down three steps to a basement door.

Inside, the light was dim, and it smelled of dirty laundry and mildew. They walked into the low-ceilinged kitchen, and the one guy, the guy who had been driving, opened the fridge, grabbed a few cans of Blue, and tossed one to each of them. The other guy disappeared into the living room, and within seconds Steppenwolf's "Magic Carpet Ride" filled the air. The one who looked like an older, weathered, meaner Charlie Brown said, "You guys live around here?" Mikhail barked out that he lived only a few blocks away, up near Rupert Street. *What an idiot,* Frank thought, *why would you give these guys any personal information?* Frank lied, said he lived in Burnaby, other side of Central Park. Mikhail couldn't figure out why he'd make up something like that. Soon they were in the living room, sitting on a low couch around a coffee table littered with the remnants of bachelor life: beer bottles, plastic mickey bottles, fast-food containers, torn-open chip bags, squashed pizza boxes, well-worn skin mags, cigarette packs, overflowing ashtrays, and stubs of candles in solidified puddles of wax. Frank and Mikhail sipped their beers and stared at each other, trying to convey silent messages under the roaring organ swells of Goldy McJohn. Frank got up to see where the two guys were and when he leaned to look into the kitchen, the guy with the catcher's-mitt face was whispering into the other guy's ear. Frank downed his beer and motioned for Mikhail to get up, move. Mikhail asked him what was going on, and Frank said he thought they should leave. They walked into the kitchen, and the two guys turned to face them. "Where ya goin'?" said the one who had asked them over. "It's late," said Frank. "We gotta get goin'." Mean Charlie Brown blocked their way to the door. "I thought you guys wanted to party? We got more beer—my pal here's even got a few lines of coke! Hell, we're just gettin' started!" Frank was lean and hard and he had his Daytons on. He pushed up close to Mean Charlie Brown, stared into rheumy eyes that looked sad, hurt. Frank called his bluff and pushed past him toward the basement door. Mikhail followed close behind. "Hang on, I'll give you a lift!" said Mean Charlie Brown, coming up behind them. "It's all right," said Frank. "We'll walk." And they climbed the three concrete steps and headed out to the street, hundreds of thousands of stars above them, benign in their distant burning. "What the fuck was that about?" Mikhail asked, taking long strides to keep up with Frank. "There's something going on there, that's all I know." They walked fast, side by side, south to 41st Avenue, and then headed east. Eight years later, Frank is nursing a beer and a vicious hangover, watching *The Six O'clock News* when a man is led from a building to a waiting van, his arms out in front of him, cuffed at the wrists, his unkempt hair falling down around his pumpkin-shaped face. Frank is stunned, almost certain he is looking at a slightly aged version of Mean Charlie Brown. Melanie would be home soon. They'd eat dinner, share some wine, play a game of backgammon, and maybe, just maybe, he'd tell her the story of Mean Charlie Brown.

Three
CATACLYSMS

Oh, to Be Affable Again

Prior to "the event," his life had been sunny and filled with promise. He had experienced the adoration of millions, both in his own country and many from abroad. He had arrived at airports to smiling, swooning crowds, many calling his name and waving. Women approached him with bouquets of flowers. There were state dinners, brandies shared with diplomats and foreign attachés; celebrities were often seen in his company. Limousine doors were opened and closed by unknown yet familiar-looking young men in suits and dark sunglasses. And it was one such young, athletic man who had placed the barrel of the gun against his abdomen and discharged two rounds. Before he hit the ground, the Secret Service guys were on his assailant, wrestling him to the ground too. But it wasn't this part of "the event" that made his sunny days dreary. No, initially there had been an expected outpouring of grief: vigils and prayers for his speedy recovery. No, it was later, when the letters and tapes surfaced—those tapes, with such incriminating words, set against a backdrop of political espionage and state secrets—that everything changed. The invitations stopped coming and the only ones who seemed to adore him as the millions had done in the past were his wife and daughter. People close to him and people he had never met before called for his resignation. This didn't bother him nearly as much as the fact that he no longer felt affable, open to almost anything.

Agreed-Upon Destinations, Agreed-Upon Times

She wore a black hat, medium brimmed, like that of a pioneer woman, and walked upright, as if the discipline of girlhood ballet classes had never left her. Some might say she walked with purpose. She thought of this often, but really it was just good posture. Today, however, was different: she really was walking with purpose, with a particular destination in mind and a specific time at which to meet her companion of the evening, a Mr. Doitz from the Planning Department who had offered to take her to the opera, something she had never done before but was certainly aware of, knew it to be something people sometimes did in the evening. She wore her large dark sunglasses so as to appear somewhat elegant, more European. And perhaps it was the darkness of the sunglasses that prevented her from noticing the car as it careered in her direction, jumped the curb, and connected solidly with her left hip, sending her through the air and to the sidewalk and up against the wall of the bank. The glasses were gone now, and she saw clearly, clearly, that her first experience of *Tosca*, Puccini's opera in three acts, would not occur today, and Mr. Doitz would be puzzled, perhaps upset, that she had not arrived at their agreed-upon destination at the agreed-upon time.

Unexpected Mechanical Difficulties

The short, slight, blond woman and her tall, slim companion parked the Mustang on a side street about a block from the hospital on Vancouver's west side. Before climbing out of the convertible, she tried—unsuccessfully—to raise the roof of the car. The tall man made weak attempts—perfunctory at best—to get the roof to rise, but he, too, was unsuccessful. He stood beside the Mustang convertible, a cold ice-blue model, bidding that they carry on with their plan, which was to visit his ailing mother who had ended up in the hospital after taking ill on a boat cruise to Alaska from her home in Tacoma, Washington. The small blonde was reluctant to leave the vehicle unattended, with the roof down—the back seat was packed with camping gear and all their belongings, as they were en route from Eugene, Oregon, to Fort McMurray, Alberta, in search of well-paying jobs. They were sharing the gas and the driving and planned to travel straight through so as not to miss out on any opportunities in the oil and gas industry. Fort Mac was, as one close friend had told them, just like the Gold Rush of the late 1800s. It was only by the sheerest of luck or fate that they had been passing through Vancouver the day after his mother had been hospitalized for a mysterious stomach ailment. He felt compelled to visit her on their one night in the west-coast Canadian city. The small, slight blonde continued to fiddle with the mechanical apparatus that controlled the raising and lowering of the car's roof, leaning deep into the workings below the folded roof material and in so doing revealing the bottom half of her buttocks and the bottom half of a black thong strap. Her tall travelling companion found these displays vulgar, somewhat tawdry—and there had been several such displays in the eleven hours they had been on the road.

After two more unsuccessful attempts to get the roof to rise and fold into place, they agreed to leave the Mustang and their belongings unattended and walk the block and a half to the hospital where his mother lay in a bed, worrying about the mystery of her condition. They did so, walking side by side, their tent and boxes fully exposed in the ice-blue Mustang at the expired parking meter on the side street in Vancouver's west-side medical neighbourhood. They failed, however, to reflect on the fact that they were in Vancouver, in November, and—amazingly—it wasn't raining.

Solemn Bob

He stood at his printing press ten hours a day, six days a week, watching the sheets shoot out the end of the small AB Dick 360 and get gently jogged by the guide arms moving slowly in and out, in and out, and stubbed out cigarette after cigarette, like a prisoner scratching days on the wall of his cell. At the stroke of the eighth hour, levers were thrown, sending the machine into idle, and out the back door of the print shop he would go, seventy-five steps to the pub and seventy-five steps back, where the first of six beer cans would burst to an accompaniment of the press's air suction, and the sheets once again began jettisoning from the ass end of the delivery chain. The beers would be gulped, drained in succession, until hour ten approached, then he'd squash the last can against his thigh and lightly lob it the two-and-a-half feet to the garbage can. Solemn Bob would then grab his coat, toss it over his shoulder—dangling by one finger—and head toward the back door. No "Good night," no "So long," no "I'm outta here," just his slumped shoulders and thin ponytail disappearing into the dark alleyway behind the shop. And Kenny G.—Print Man #2—would look out over the production room, out over the folders, collators, binding equipment, cans of inks and solvents, reams and reams of paper, the sloppy piles of clean wash-up rags, and whisper: "Good night, sweet prince."

An Impulse

They'd been hearing sirens for about five minutes before they realized that the source of those sirens—emergency response vehicles—was coming down their road, past their place of business, and heading down under the bridge toward the waters of False Creek. Curiosity got the better of them, and they strolled toward the island—which is what people called the area, but it was, in fact, only an isthmus—to see if they could see what the bustle was all about. Fire? Car accident? Heart attack? They walked casually down under the bridge that was, at its crest, one hundred feet from the water, and were halfway to the dock area when they saw it. A jumper. A person—a woman, it appeared to be—in a crumpled little pile, much like the Wicked Witch of the West when she melted. They were prevented by medics and police from moving any closer, but from where they stood they could see that the jumper's eyes were open, staring straight ahead. She hadn't cleared the rocks, never even hit the water. They returned to work and mused about the event for the rest of the day, wondered about it, that impulse to jump. Years later, Lance, one of the workers who had walked down under the bridge that day to sate his curiosity and saw the woman in her crumpled and broken end, had met a woman who had once jumped off the other end of the same steel-girder bridge and who had, obviously, survived. She had done it "on an impulse," she said. She was having a horrible few days—a relationship had ended, she'd bounced her rent cheque, and just that morning she'd been fired from her job. An impulse. Before she knew it, she was over the rail and soaring. She hit the water, was rescued by two kayakers, and suffered only minor injuries. When she asked her psychiatrist, "But why?" she was told not to dwell on it, to move on, and accept that it was only an *impulse.*

Head in Oven

No one had seen him in months, and then it was discovered that he had moved to Prince George. No one knew why exactly, but it was presumed he had moved north for love or adventure. Or just a "Go up north, work hard, make a lot of money" sort of thing. But it was also known that he'd been involved in minor drug dealing in the city, though nothing serious. It was rumoured that, perhaps, he was running from someone or something, though this rumour was never substantiated. And he was a strikingly attractive man with a headful of black curls and a strong Roman nose, so it was all the more surprising when it was discovered that he had killed himself in Prince George—turned on the gas and put his head and upper torso in the oven. It was never determined what he was seeking in Prince George or what Prince George may have held for him, but it was certain that he had turned on the gas and put his head in the oven, for that is how and where he had been discovered.

Dr. Angel

He was slight, smocked in white, and when he cupped Barry's testicles in his cool palm he made him feel as if he were, for the moment, being held in the palm of God. Maybe not God in its entirety, but certainly in the grace and company of an emissary of the divine. Cool, gentle, slow, and knowledgeable manipulation—not the sort of touch that brought to mind times behind the bleachers or in the back seat of a car—mingled under the fluorescent glare with a cool, empathetic air that was only ever found in the truly pious or those so completely at peace with the idea of death that they could do nothing more than try to transport others over that bridge. He circumvented the lump with near weightless rolls, tilts, and the slightest of pressure. After several moments, like drifting in an open skiff, the Angel of Fate made the proclamation, as if decrying a rebuild of the *Titanic*—"No, cancer does not live here." Barry's underwear and jeans were pulled up and rearranged around his buttocks, genitals, and thighs. He asked the doc how he could be so certain, how he could know for sure. "I see it every day," said the slim defrocked man with the cool, dry hands. "*This* is not *it*." And in the anteroom, the waiting room, where no muzak played and the air conditioner hummed, sat eight to ten middle-aged men, staring into a vanishing point somewhere above the coffee table that held the scattered magazines, silently awaiting their turn with Dr. Angel. And as Barry came out of the inner room and passed through the small group of stern-faced men, he jerked his chin down slightly in a congenial gesture, but none of the men seemed to notice, and he felt the way he imagined the small fish do, the ones that fit through the net.

Going Under

The anesthesiologist says, "Okay, I want you to count back from one hundred." Why do they say that? Why don't they say, *I want you to count back from two.* He barely gets the word *one* from his lips and a coal-black curtain slides across his eyes, over his conscious mind, and he is plunged into a lightless void of disembodied voices and sounds, zipping in and out in a formless realm, a murky bardo. He has a sense of place but also the dark aloneness of deep space, like a child locked in a closet, yet no fear grips him. Time is an illusion, consciousness a hypnosis. He wanders the black passageways as if in a vast and empty mansion. *Where is everyone? Where am I?* It is not so much a plummet—like Renton takes through the floor at Madame Superior's in Danny Boyle's film *Trainspotting*—as a drift in a starless heaven, an atomized soul, floating like a vapour, etherealized. He now walks with the Thief of Sleep. A voice echoes, a cold marble utterance: "Mr. Markun?" "Yes?" he says. Then, as if from the bottom of an abandoned mine shaft, he asks: "Am I supposed to wake up now?" A "Yes" whispers down to him. Then comes the ascension: up the black shaft toward the sky and the painful return to the world.

Not Good

He made him think—immediately upon seeing him—of Chief Bromden from *One Flew Over the Cuckoo's Nest* or, more accurately, of the actor Will Sampson as he embodied the character of Chief in the film. When he thundered down the sidewalk outside the historic Lee Building at the intersection of Main Street and Broadway in Mount Pleasant and pulled up short in front of the publisher, who had just stepped out of the historic building for a bit of fresh air and to smoke a tightly rolled cigarette of Drum tobacco, he was—the publisher, that is—as they like to say in such circumstances, taken aback. The hulking, imposing figure of a man looked down at the short publisher, litre bottle of red wine just lowered from his lips, and asked: "How do I look?" But before the publisher could expel the smoke that was roiling around in his lungs, "Chief" was off and running again, in large, lumbering strides, litre bottle now tilted vertical and tight to his lips, being pursued by a shorter, stockier guy, who was yelling, "Hey! Gimme some of that!" Had he waited for the publisher to gasp his smoke and grab a breath, the publisher would have told him, *Not good!* But he was gone as fast as he'd appeared, running along Broadway, laughing and evading his pursuer. He also had what appeared to be a slash across his throat, nearly ear to ear, that had been, it appeared, stapled—not stitched—together with what looked like large box staples, and no, it did not look good, did not look right. And now he—not Chief, not Will Sampson, but the guy who only looked like the character of Chief Bromden as played by Will Sampson—was running down East Broadway in Vancouver with his stapled neck, alive as any man had ever been.

Gulf War I

He has escaped the madness of his Main Street apartment. No more screaming fights from the City Centre Motel, no more hoots and hollers and smashing bottles at 3 a.m. He is now in the safe and comforting embrace of the housing co-op. He has waited years to be offered a suite. He took the call from someone on the membership committee who apologized about the size of the ground-level bachelor unit and how he could put his name on the list to "transfer" suites, and that it might be only a year or two before he could apply for a one-bedroom, when he interjected, "I'll take it!" Now here he is, flat on his back on his compressed futon, staring at the ceiling, surrounded by unpacked boxes, feeling as if he has just been released from prison and given a massive injection of Clonazepam. He is calm, completely at peace. What is not at peace is his fourteen-inch, black-and-white Sony TV, its screen filled with grainy images of the Gulf War—burning tanks, sooty flames from Kuwaiti oil fields, Hornets and F-16As and F-15C bombers drifting through smoky skies as Scud missiles flash in white blotches across the bottom of the screen. And in the morning, he will dig through the boxes to find his cutting mat, his T-square, his waxer, and X-Acto knives and get going on a new issue of his magazine. His hands will get smeared with ink—not blood or oil—and he'll set up his drafting table in front of the window with the Chinese paper blind and let the north-shore breeze drift his way. And he will lay down the columns of type, wax the PMTs of photos and art onto the flats, the rebel words of creators—not destroyers—and do what he can in his tiny bachelor apartment, make his small moves and shakes in the world, strive to make a positive difference, and at one-thirty precisely he will walk the two blocks to his favourite diner, Slickity Jim's Chat 'N' Chew, for a burger and small salad, and join the troops there while they continue in their mission to—as the sign above the pass-through window says—MAKE LUNCH, NOT WAR!

The Happy Diner

Alice is a Canada Post lifer: she has survived three strikes, forced arbitration, contract disputes, five federal government changes, benefit erosion, and seventeen years of graveyard shift. She walks the floor of the Happy Diner in her knee-high gumboots and tartan skirt and tells anyone who will listen—as well as anyone who merely makes eye contact—about the issues of the day. "I told my supervisor, we can't go on like this. Inflation is killing us… Do you know we've been without a contract now for thirty-two months? And no one cares… They all like getting their mail, but no one really cares. We bring the mail to every corner of this country, and what do they do for me now?" Her attention is diverted as the door to the Happy Diner opens and in walks the Silent Man, with his top hat, dyed black hair, waxed moustache, and walking stick. He is six-two and appears to have stepped out of a Wild West movie. He lives in the rooming house along Main by the barber shop, next to the porn cinema. Alice tilts her head in his direction but does not say hello, though she most assuredly knows his name, but he rarely engages with others. He gets his cup of black coffee and makes his way to a booth by the window. Alice turns back to the young publisher, pats one palm onto the other. "And you've got the minimum wage. Hasn't gone up in three years. Six-fifty—how can anyone live on that? You might as well lie down in the road and die!" Then the Twins walk in. They bounce on the balls of their feet, always popping their heads up, giraffe-like, as if looking for someone on the run, someone who is hiding from them. All times of the day and night they appear, prancing through the café, never sitting or eating. They don't work regular jobs, keep regular hours. They are vestiges of old Main Street, from a time when the area was strictly working class, lower class, maybe even welfare class—a hood of poverty, violence, drugs, and prostitution. And he, the publisher, represents the current invasion of young professionals, artists, and hipsters taking over their hood. He, as they would see it, is part of the problem. The publisher is waiting for an author, an activist/street poet who carries his own engrained poverty mentality from his battered childhood days in Michigan, when there was never enough food on the table. To this early layered imprinting, add years of addiction, several suicide attempts, and cycles of domestic violence. The publisher will buy him breakfast—pancakes and bacon—and watch him methodically cut the pancakes into one-inch squares before putting down his knife and stabbing them with a fork, wolfing them as if someone might just as quickly take the plate away again. Then in shuffles the Bunny Lady from the apartments upstairs, wearing her pink nightgown and bunny slippers, looking befuddled, like she thinks she maybe walked through the wrong door and should be next door in the lobby of the Historic Lee Building and is wondering why there are men in white hats behind a counter cooking food…and who are all these people in the lobby? Where did they come from? What's their backstory? Outside the big plate-glass windows facing Broadway, Madras Madras, in his powder-blue suit, saunters to the door. Madras Madras, the notary public with the funny name. It must be twelve-fifteen, for he is like clockwork. The young publisher takes his financial papers to Madras Madras to have his income verification statement notarized. Madras Madras stops just inside the door, head hanging, almost perpendicular to the floor, and smiles at the publisher sitting in his booth. He leans on his cane, asks, "How is business?" The publisher shrugs. "Same battle, different day." Madras Madras blinks slowly and nods. "Keep going!" His backstory—at least a part of it—is knowable, for it is tattooed on his wrist: blue numbers, crudely drawn. Five single-needle digits, seen once by the publisher as Madras Madras reached for his notary stamp, the sleeve cuff of his suit jacket sliding up his arm. *Thump, thump,* as the stamp hit the papers. "You need to make more money!" he drawled, smiling at the young publisher over his spectacles. Behind him, three filing cabinets with towering piles of bulging file folders loomed like smokestacks.

The Meaning of Work

He is on the #3 Main Street bus heading downtown. It's November, raining, and the bus is packed. Fogged windows are briskly swept with fingertips as riders try to get a view beyond the steamed-up transportation tube in which they are temporarily trapped. Frank is on the bench seat by the back doors, reading Malatesta's *Anarchy* and knocking knees with his co-riders every time the bus decelerates. At Terminal the brake hoses hiss and clear, and the riders sit for a few minutes while the driver gets back on schedule. A teen across from Frank nudges his friend and snorts in Frank's direction, as if to say, "Look what the nerd is reading." A few passengers get anxious, leaning into the aisle, looking toward the driver, wondering why the bus isn't moving. The brake lines let out another long gasp of air and the vehicle starts to pull away when they all hear: "WAIT! WAIT!" The driver hits the brakes and the strap-hangers lurch toward the front of the bus, then sway back to an upright position. A guy in his late twenties gets on. He wears a filthy white parka with a fur collar and is soaked from the rain. His face is tomato red. Heavy-set, out of shape, purple Crocs on his feet. He pushes his way to the back, forcing himself between people in the aisle. He stops in front of Frank and stares down at him as if he expects Frank to give up his seat. Frank says, "Why don't you sit over there," and points at the one vacant seat on the bus: centre spot on the rear bench. One of the teens across the aisle says, "Get your fat ass outta my face, ya fuckin' retard!" and gives the guy a light shove. A woman in a corporate white power suit, briefcase on lap, stops tapping at her phone and looks up. "You can't say that! Can't use that word anymore! *Inappropriate.*" The teen whispers something to his friend and they both laugh. The red-faced guy is wiping his brow and fidgeting, and Frank lightly taps his arm and points again at the empty seat, and the guy shuffles crablike a couple of feet down the aisle and sits. The bus jerks away from the curb as the driver calls out, "Chinatown! Next stop, Chinatown!" The guy in the dirty parka appears increasingly agitated and suddenly starts beating his forehead with closed fists, like he's pounding a drum. He exclaims loudly a rhetorical question, still valid and largely unanswered: "WHAT IS THE MEANING OF WORK!" Some passengers turn and stare, while others keep their gaze fixed on their phones. The woman in white snaps up like a meerkat, glares at the parka guy: "Do you want to get put back in? If not, you better get control of yourself." He goes silent, looking down at his hands that are now folded on his lap. Errico Malatesta, the Italian anarchist, struggled with such questions, sought passionately to free the working class from the yoke of mandatory labour and state oppression. The bus is now approaching Main and Hastings, the Downtown Eastside, and Frank dings the bell and rises. He has a meeting with a poet. He is planning to publish the man's first book. He is an activist and social justice warrior and his concerns resemble Malatesta's and the parka guy's, and Frank and the poet will drink strong coffee in a café and talk at length about—among other things—the meaning of work.

The Handshake

Frank knew it was a ruse the second the guy extended his beefy mitt toward the kid and said, "So, no hard feelings?" He wanted to yell, "Don't fall for it!" but it was too late. It was an old con he'd experienced as an adolescent. Old guys—dock workers, truck drivers, guys that worked with their hands—thought it was clever, funny. Only a rube, a sucker, would fall for it. It told them whether you were "street" or some privileged kid from the rich side of town. Frank could see that this kid was not street and he knew what was about to happen. The kid put forth his limp arm while his other rested across the shoulders of his teenage girlfriend. The bus stopped and the back doors accordioned in a slap at the exact moment the redneck's thick, meaty palm arced up and into the kid's face—as if executing a joke with a cream pie. But there was no cream pie, just the disturbing sound of flesh slapping on flesh, and the guy was gone, down the steps and off the bus, laughing hard before the kid or any other passenger on the bus could elicit shock or outrage. The teen sat red-faced and sucker-punched, stunned and blinking, staring straight ahead and out the window at the pedestrians walking along West Broadway.

Samurai

He had fooled around with Jerry's wife; that was true. Okay, it was stupid, but it didn't mean anything. Okay, it did, but not much of anything, not enough to have everyone who knew them act the way they were acting. He was going to go see Jerry and clear the air. Clear the air about Claire. If possible, make amends and get some closure so everyone could get on with things. As he approached the front door of Jerry's little one-storey dilapidated rental on 12th Avenue off Main, the door burst open and Jerry sprung out wearing a tattered sky-blue terrycloth bathrobe and swinging a samurai sword. He—Bobby, the adulterer—could not help but laugh, Jerry looking so much like Rahad Jackson from *Boogie Nights* when he bursts out of the bedroom, levelling a shotgun at the three ass-clowns who are scheming to rip him off. And as Bobby is laughing and Jerry is not, it occurs to Jerry that Bobby may be laughing *at* him, laughing at *their* situation, about poor sad-sack Jerry being all twisted out of shape because his wife had a brief and stupid fling with his best friend. And so Jerry runs him through, skewers Bobby with his samurai sword that he purchased only a month earlier from a pawnshop on Main Street, not really knowing why he was buying such a thing. And Jerry watches Bobby fall backwards off the sword, landing flat on his back on the narrow concrete path between the two yellowing patches of lawn that the landlord rarely cut. As he is bleeding out on the cracked and bumpy sidewalk, Bobby still can't understand what all the fuss is about. And as he's lying there, looking up, he notices that Jerry's robe is wide open and he's nude beneath it. And Bobby also notices that Jerry shaves his pubes, and as he drifts toward unconsciousness, he wonders, *Why?*

The Hit

It's an East Van two-bedroom bungalow. He's checked and double-checked the address, consulted the city registry, and is confident he has the right place. He's done his homework, he's no amateur. He hops off the bus and takes a jaunt along Victoria Drive for a couple hundred yards, then heads down 50th Avenue and jags down the alleyway just past the corner lot. Some of the alleyways, like this one, are still unpaved, and the rocks and gravel crunch under his shoes as he makes his way west past the garages and carports and gardens of beans, raspberry bushes, and tall sunflowers. He steps over a shallow ditch, grabs the gate, and reaches up and over to feel for the latch. He opens the gate, steps through cautiously, and leaves it ajar behind him. He crosses the yard in large strides, beneath the branches of a big cherry tree, and steps down three short stairs to the basement door. The weight swings in his jacket pocket as he tries the handle. Locked. He takes the steps to the back door. It's open, covered by a screen door. Hot air from the house blows over his face. He opens the screen door and steps into the kitchen. Hearing voices, he moves swiftly toward the living room. "Hello?" calls a woman's voice, and a blonde in cut-offs and a tank top steps into the doorway. He barely has the gun pulled from his pocket as he lets off the first round and the blonde goes backwards and down onto the oval rag rug when, to his right, the bathroom door bursts out and a crazy-looking, curly-haired bearded guy with bangles on each wrist lunges for him. *Darryl?* He lets off a second round and is pretty sure he gets the guy in the upper thigh before Darryl slams into him like a three-hundred-pound linebacker. His head hits the edge of the fridge as they spin around and slam hard against the kitchen counter. A third explosion erupts from his clenched hand, and he is certain this time that the big guy takes a direct hit, upper left quadrant, and he goes down hard against the door jamb leading to one of the bedrooms. It didn't unfold how he imagined, never does. Only supposed to be one, just this "Darryl," who, he presumes now, lies at his feet. He leaves the way he came and tries not to think about the girl: he'll have plenty of time to feel bad about that.

Opium

Doug Colchester was always the first: first to smoke pot, first to thwang a violin bow across the strings of his open-body Gibson ES-335, first to bring us seal-free cigarettes, first to open a tinfoil package of hashish, first to drop LSD, and first to unveil opium—the Dragon Lady, the Stealer of Dreams. Black and soft, it fell apart like compressed roe, smouldered slow like damp leaves on the orange end of a hot cigarette, the thick grey smoke swirling up, a genie from a lamp. Doug inhaled it slowly up each nostril, smirked, and extended his arms to whoever else wanted to lean in, nose down. Three of them sampled the drug and felt universally nonplussed with the effects. It seemed to do very little to their mental state, their general euphoria, nor did they notice any other unexpected effects of the drug. They sat in three upholstered armchairs around a low, round coffee table. Every few moments it felt as though the angles of their chairs changed, but no one seemed to move. "I'm not even high," one of them thought he said. They sat in silence, realized it wasn't the chairs shifting, but the walls. "Did you say something?" another one asked, but neither of the other two was aware of anyone having said anything. "Yes," said a voice, disembodied or within the table, none of them could really tell.

Spicy Menace

It was mid-July and blisteringly hot in Willy's three-storey brick walk-up. His friend Raoul would soon be by for dinner and drinks, and he was behind in his prep. The little bulk store on Main had sold him the spices and other necessary ingredients for the soup he planned to make—lemongrass, galanga, kaffir lime leaves, fish sauce, lime juice, and firecracker red chili paste. The buzzer rang and his white cat, Tyke, leapt a foot in the air before vanishing down the hall. Raoul came through the apartment door minutes later, plunked a six-pack of Molson's on the counter, and immediately pried two from their plastic yokes, popped a tab, and extended his arm to Willy—"Salud!" Cans clicked and gulps were taken. Willy resumed his chopping and dicing as the opening bars of Zappa's "Peaches En Regalia" filled the room. Raoul lit a smoke in defiance of recent anti-smoking laws, folded his arms like Bob Hope, just as Tyke zoomed through the living room, bounced off the wall, and disappeared back down the hall toward the washroom. Willy continued to sauté the ingredients, adding the hockey-puck-sized can of chili paste to the sizzling pot. Halfway through their second beer, he dished up two large bowls of tom yum gai. He yanked the carriage window open wide to help with the stifling heat and noticed that the oscillating fan blade appeared to be going backwards. Raoul took a spoonful of the soup, and Willy watched his face get redder and redder, beads of sweat bursting forth on his forehead. Tyke zoomed back into the room, stopped, stared at them for a moment, her tail whipping back and forth, then was gone again. "That's pretty hot, Willy," Raoul said between gasps of breath and swigs of beer. The crazy cat, named in honour of Kerouac's cat, tore back through the kitchen, bounced off the wall beside the fridge, and ripped across the lino toward the exterior wall, where she leapt up, intent on pushing off the wall—as she had done so many times before—only to sail straight out the wide-open window. "Wow!" said Raoul, and Willy wasn't sure if he was referring to the cat that had just disappeared out the window or the tom yum gai, which was, apparently, "too hot."

Rose's Place

They caught the blues jam at the Yale Hotel and are now migrating up Granville to the Royal Hotel where cheap, sudsy beer is always "on special." Chester and Pasquale move slowly from the glaring outdoors through the heavy entrance door edged with battered brass moulding and wait just inside for their eyes to adjust to the gloom. Then they amble, cool as cucumbers, into the depths of the sparsely populated beer parlour. Chester slips his aviator sunglasses up on top of his head and points at a table halfway up the bar, exclaiming, "There!" He drops his ubiquitous shoulder bag—big enough to hold a small tea kettle and a forty-pounder of vodka—and lights up a smoke before settling in, back to the wall as always, and signals the waiter for *three* beers. He does not like waiting between beers. It is disruptive to the flow of conversation, and in a "world of crumbling beauty" what else do they have? Chester can rant on, holding court and entertaining an entire table for hours, as he often does, his landslide mouth working, wild spinning eyes topped by a self-barbered mane of feral black ringlets that drop like garter snakes to his shoulders. And the words tumble a mile a minute at Pasquale—short and wiry, tongue lolling out every few minutes in an attempt to keep up with the torrent. He is a sort of dingo at your heels: always nipping but never really sinking the teeth into the shank of the convo. Hours pass and glass after glass of sudsy lager are consumed before Rose and Walter arrive and approach the small but boisterous table of Chester Hoyne and Pasquale Benzito. Rose and Chester seem to know each other from some past time, and hugs ensue, Pasquale shaking the hand of Walter as another round lands on the red terry-cloth tabletop. Thick, dimpled beer mugs are hoisted and clinked as country music erupts from the jukebox. More rounds, dancing, and cig after cig puffed and extinguished in the overflowing ashtray, the clock slow-sliding toward midnight, when Rose suggests they take the party back to their place. "Yes!" howls Chester, and the pints are downed and off-sales procured and they are out the doors and onto the Granville strip, taking the short hike over to Helmcken Street. Walter pushes open the door of their small, subsidized housing unit, says, "Make yerself at home!" Beer cans are popped, smokes lit. Rose throws Hank Williams on the turntable and "Jambalaya" hop-skips through the air, filling the small room. The moon now over the yardarm, Pasquale is so sotted he can barely speak but somehow manages a sloppy version of the two-step with Rose while Walter laughs and claps. Chester has now gone mostly silent, shifting from "life of the party" to a distant dwarf star, silent and brooding in a dark corner of his own universe. Pasquale side-steps to the kitchen table they've gathered around, grabs his beer, and raises it in a toast to Chester. "This reminds me of the night you and Miss Lee got in the big fight about moving to Richmond and you put your fist through the wall. Remember that?" Chester takes a long, slow drag on his smoke and looks up at Pasquale. "You don't know *shit*," he says as Rose thunders in from the living room. "We're going to the store!" "Need more beer!" cries Walter, waiting at the door. "I know a guy!" "And I'm gonna grab some snacks and smokes. Be right back!" They are out the door, and Pasquale slowly sinks into the chair across the table from Chester, whose eyes now resemble dying embers in a firepit. *Hello, Darkness, my old…* Pasquale thinks it but does not say it. Thinks it would be funny, but tells himself, *Don't do it…* but it is as if he *did* say the words, or telepathically sent them through his eyes and into the black hole of Chester's brain, for he erupts like a grizzly in attack mode and is over the table and on Pasquale in seconds. To the floor they crash in a flurry of limbs and discordant breaking sounds, Pasquale grabbed by the hair and sent backwards, hard, into the wall. Chester is kneeling, looming above him, staring down, breathing hard. No words are spoken and Pasquale realizes he is now looking into the eyes of madness. Did he lose consciousness? He's not sure, perhaps momentarily, for he suddenly realizes he is now alone, prone on the floor, neck and head tilted up against the wall, tufts of hair sliding down his face like corn silk. He hears voices, and Rose and Walter step through the already open door. Rose: "Oh, my god!" Walter: "What the fuck!" Rose steps into the trashed arena of her once cute kitchen set-up. "What happened?" Pasquale decides to lie. He sees now that a leg of the kitchen table gave way and the floor is littered with cans, bottles, cigarette butts, and broken glass. He needs a way out. "Chester went crazy! Went nuts. Exploded on me out of the blue, for no fucking reason!" Rose and Walter stand silent, surveying the ruin. Pasquale feels two centuries of settler guilt descend. Whitey always saying sorry. Then he says it, standing by the door, about to leave: "I'm sorry this happened." Neither Rose nor Walter say a word. Rose has already started sweeping up the mess. Pasquale heads down the red-carpeted hallway toward the Exit sign and down the stairs to a side entrance that ejects him onto a walkway leading to Seymour Street. He skitters like the rat he is toward Davie, then down, headed for Mainland. He ducks into an alley and walks through what was once the old warehousing district, heading for Nelson Street and maybe a Cambie bus, or to walk the bridge over False Creek and climb the hill toward City Hall, to the safety and sanctuary of his Mount Pleasant room.

Arco Hotel

It was well past closing time, but there was no shortage of booze. Marty had brought them all back to his place, a room he shared with several other people. It was only a three-minute walk from the Grand Union Hotel on Hastings, just around the corner onto Pender, so they were there in no time, with paper bags of off-sale beer, in his crowded room on the second floor. The nicotine-stained white curtains appeared to be melting off their rails and the institutional green walls hummed with the trapped voices of the past hundred years. Marty popped beer cans and passed them around the smoke-filled combination living room, kitchen, and bedroom. A large green-and-white parrot in a domed cage bobbed its head up and down, and Violet—who also shared the room—hooted and danced to a Stones song she had trapped in her head—"Ain't too proud to beg, sweet darlin'!" She swung her arms out from her hips, like little wings, like Jagger doing his rooster dance. Marty cackled and shimmied up behind her. A guy named Ron yelled, "Somebody spike a spliff!" and almost instantly a fresh cloud of smoke billowed toward the ceiling. The parrot bobbed its head more feverishly, said, "It's a par-ty! *Brrawwwk!* It's a par-ty!" and everybody laughed. Marty's mother, Eunice, sat in the big armchair that filled the middle of the room and every ten minutes or so would say, "Marty, be a sweetheart and bring your mother a drink!" and Marty would just keep gyrating beside Violet. Ron exhaled a gust of pot smoke, leaned over with the joint extended, and said, "What'd ya say your name was again? … Marty! Get your mom a beer!" It was only then that Bobby realized that he didn't know any of these people, couldn't remember what he was doing there, where he was, or why he was there, and that he was also extremely high. The parrot stared down at him, its pebble eye jerking up, then down, and Bobby was sure it said, "Get outta Dodge! Get outta Dodge!" And after struggling to find the door to the hallway, he slipped, caught the toe of his boot on the metal weather stripping covering the edge of the top step, and was down the twenty-plus stairs to the glass-and-aluminum entrance door to the Arco Hotel in seconds. After a few moments of desolate stillness, he pulled himself upright, pushed the door open, and staggered out onto Pender Street. "Hey, are you all right?" he heard from behind him, but he kept walking—slowly, determinedly—east toward Main Street.

Casino

They are in the backroom—the locked "vault"—counting the money from the blackjack tables. Methodically opening and dumping the cash boxes, emptying them onto long metal tables before tilting and pointing the open end of the box up toward the security camera so it can be recorded that the box is, indeed, devoid of bills. As the handfuls of twenties, fifties, and hundreds are fed into the bill counter, it occurs to him that this is the spot—this exact room—where they will come when the heist takes place. They will somehow bust through the reinforced security door, and he'll be face to face with a pump shotgun and balaclavaed faces. Here, this room where Frank and Kenny sit at 2:15 a.m. on a Saturday night, working the casino so the non-profit they both volunteer for can get their small cut of the B.C. gaming revenues. They count all the boxes from this round—six or seven—and are then escorted back onto the floor to circulate until their assistance is needed again. Outside the thick greenish windows, Frank can see that it is now snowing. Heavy, fat flakes drift by like chunks of white ash. By the time they settle the cash and are released from duty, the buses will no longer be running and it will be impossible to get a cab. Kristy runs up to Frank and says she has to go, right away, if she wants to have any chance of making it home to Surrey. She is the treasurer for their non-profit and dedicates many unpaid hours to keeping their books straight. Frank tells her to go, to get a receipt if she takes a cab so she can get reimbursed at the next meeting. Kenny strides up on Frank's left, holding a styrofoam cup of coffee and spinning the stir stick. He says he just ran into an ex at the roulette table. The affair hadn't ended well, but she suggested they go for coffee. He isn't sure it's a good idea. A guy the size and build of a linebacker dressed in a starched white shirt and a black bow tie approaches them quickly. He darts his index finger at each of them, says, "You, you, come with me!" And they are off again, back on duty, to help with who-knows-what. The wheels of commerce never stop spinning, and outside the window the big cottony flakes continue to swirl by. They will be here at least another hour. Maybe two. Kenny says he might go for coffee after, he'll see how he feels at the end of the night. Cheryl—the ex—smiles as they pass the roulette table. Kenny smirks and keeps walking, staying close to the linebacker, and Frank isn't far behind. They hear a loud bang and some commotion, and Frank freezes, thinks, *This is it, here they come,* as a staff person bursts through the lobby doors with a huge brass luggage rack and crosses the room in front of them, heading for the elevators. "Okay, you two, this way," says the supervisor, and off they go, toward a door in the far corner of the room that no doubt leads to another hidden counting room. After an hour and fifteen of counting and recounting (the first balance was off by $3.70), they are stumbling out onto Main Street and darkened blocks on the outer edges of Chinatown. The roads are hardly cleared, and a salt truck goes by on the other side of the street. Frank decides he'll walk home. He lives in Mount Pleasant and it won't take him much more than forty, forty-five minutes to climb the slow grade from False Creek to Tenth Avenue. Kenny lights a smoke, says he might go meet her, but he's still not sure. He waves goodbye to Frank, holding his smoke cupped in his hand to protect it from the wet flakes falling all around them. Frank watches him turn and head off toward the Carnegie Centre and his room at Harbour Light, but then, abruptly, he turns onto Pender Street and disappears into Chinatown.

Men in Black

Cindy, a dead ringer for Squeaky Fromme of the Charlie Manson gang, stood above Carter and asked if she should get more beer. "Sure," he said, "get us all another round." She smiled and waited. He handed her two twenties, then the guy beside Carter put a hand on his arm and carried on with the story he'd been telling him. "They've replaced all my fillings with transmitters...they know exactly where I am every second of the day." No one at the table had ever seen this guy before tonight. Well, later, long-haired Ed said he saw him once or twice at the Alcazar Hotel over on Homer. "They want me to do surveillance, but I won't do it! I may have to get all my teeth pulled!" He claimed "they" were the Men in Black. They'd abducted him and implanted something in his brain... He could feel it...could hear them talking to him. Others at the table raised their eyebrows, rolled their eyes, and continued talking hockey, upcoming concerts, and an alternative writing mag one of them was planning to start. However, Carter couldn't turn away. "Of course," the guy continued, "no one believes me. It's so crazy, it's the perfect cover!" They drank beer for a while longer, then the band came on, and the place started to fill up. Carter went to the tight bathroom and squeezed in at one of the urinals, and when he came back to the table the guy was gone. Cindy said he had just suddenly got up and left. Carter looked to the bar, the long narrow bar that ran nearly the length of the club, with its toy train running on a track overhead, and there, at the far end, leaning on one folded arm each were a pair of guys in black suits and sunglasses. They didn't appear to be drinking, but just stood there, surveying the scene. Then Cindy distracted him with something about a manuscript she had given him over a year ago and wanted to know if he had ever read it. And after a long pull on his pint and licking the foam from his moustache, he glanced toward the bar, only to find the men in black were gone.

Her Ship Had Sailed (or, Not in Vogue)

The Polish writer and his wife were semi-celebrities among their small circle of friends and the literati who lived in the "ethnic enclave" of their city. He had written two collections of stories and a slim volume of critical essays. The stories had received a warm reception, with complimentary comparisons to the work of Heinrich Böll, Robert Walser, and Jorge Luis Borges. There were rumours—*murmurs*, really—that his work would soon be added to the syllabi of a number of influential professors of literature. What was of some concern among the literati was the level of neglect earned by the work of the Polish writer's wife, who, it was rumoured—no, *acknowledged*—had edited all the stories her husband had penned. Of particular dismay was that her screenplay, based on the life of Jane Eyre, the protagonist of Charlotte Brontë's novel, remained unproduced. Some said—no, *rumoured*—that she did not handle rejection well, and this may have contributed to her limited success. Others said it might simply be a symptom of the times: films based on nineteenth-century literature and the themes inherent therein were simply no longer in vogue.

The Moaning

The sound comes at him—*to him*—from forty feet away. It is the sound he imagines one might make if one has been gut-shot or stabbed in the abdomen, all vital organs somehow intact and one has been left to bleed out slowly. Sitting in his reading chair in his ground-floor suite, he hears it and waits. He waits for the sirens that he is sure will come, the emergency response team that will thunder across the carpeted lobby with their life-saving gear and chirping walkie-talkies. But nothing comes, just the moaning. Soon his door is open a crack, and he is peering out before his slippered feet pad the floral Tabriz carpet of the hallway in search of the source of the wounded-animal sound. He is surprised to find himself alone in the halls, no other curious faces peering from cracked doorways, no one else concerned about the deep, guttural utterances seeping through the walls. He is down the hall and standing in the lobby at the base of the first flight of stairs, looking up. He raises his foot to the first step, feels the thick underlay compress beneath his weight. Up he goes, each step silent, his hand inching along the bannister as he rises to the second floor. Halfway down the hall, he passes the fire extinguisher in its small glass box, the fire-alarm bell a red frisbee on the ceiling above. Then the moaning again, loud and close. He stares at the laminated brown door of the apartment from which he is certain the sound is emitting. He leans an ear to the door, listens, forgets to breathe. He raises a hand to knock, his frozen fist inches away from the door, then backs away slowly, as if he'd never heard a thing. Outside, from the darkened courtyard, the heavy November rain smacks against the thick leaves of the bigleaf maples, and below, unseen and untouched by most, is a slick, slimy brown layer of former life.

Look Me in the Eyes

She glides toward him from the vegetable section of the Robson Street Public Market. Thin, gaunt, sunken eyes on him, moving with intent, as if carrying a message for him, and him alone. Through the crowded aisles and coming straight at him. Even at ten feet away, he can see she is dying, terminally ill—cancer? AIDS? She is close to the end and she knows it, and she knows that he knows it. He expects to be hit up for spare change and starts digging in his pockets for coins. And then, between the eggplants and the warty cucumbers, she stops in her tracks, not two feet from him, and stares, deep and cold, massive pale grey eyes, and then he knows it is not money she wants. She needs to be seen, needs someone to *see* her and not turn away, not leave the room when Death is quietly packing its suitcase.

Fishbowl

One is in pyjamas, the other a bathrobe—"he" in the pjs; "she" in the bathrobe. He has her by the hair, and she has a fistful of his pyjama top, and they are swinging each other around the room like a ballroom two-step gone terribly wrong. From the street they look like crazed combatants in a—as if competing in a—new, twisted reality TV show—*Domestic Dispute*, or maybe *Breaking Up Is Hard to Do*. He swings and slaps her hard, and she gives it back with a closed fist to the side of his head. The two observers—Bradley Dormant and Cicily Sidetracker—stop dead in their tracks on the sidewalk outside the building. They are stunned, gobsmacked, bewildered by the donnybrook they are witnessing behind the huge ground-floor plate-glass living room window. Around the lovers go in another flurry of blows, her bathrobe falling open, a pendulous breast swaying into view. From behind Brad and Cicily comes a passerby, a man of action with a large knapsack upon his back. He bounds across the lawn and slaps the window of the apartment with the palm of his hand—"HEY!—YOU!—STOP THAT!" The couple, previously engaged in free-for-all combat, freeze and, for the first time, realize they are visible to the witnessing eyes of the outside world, all who pass by on their side street just off Main in the Mount Pleasant neighbourhood. They can now see, at this very moment, that they have attracted a small audience. The gobsmacked couple observing are doubly gobsmacked by the action—swift, decisive engagement—exhibited by their fellow observer. The spell is broken. The combatants release their grips and drift to their respective corners, casting aspersions, pointing fingers, accusing one another of a litany of shortcomings. Within minutes, the police pull up, a social worker in tow, and the questioning begins. The fighters say it's nothing, just a little argument, they just want to go to bed. Their children are asleep in the next room. "CHILDREN?" asks the social worker. This changes everything. The social worker becomes stern, cold, tells the couple that one of them will have to spend the night elsewhere. "Where? Where will I go?" the woman asks. Mr. Pyjamas decides he will go, and the cops escort him away. The Man of Action turns and looks at the gobsmacked Dormant and Sidetracker, as if to say: *See, that's how it's done. That's what "taking action" looks like.*

Quake

They are sitting on the couch watching *Six Feet Under* when he hears the grinding, feels the reverberations, like a sixteen-wheeler locking up its brakes and skidding down 18th Avenue. That's what it sounds like... but why would a big rig be coming down their street at 11 p.m.? They look at each other, and then he glances up, certain he sees the windows in their old wood frames pucker and bulge as if they might blow out in a pop of tiny glass fragments. He leaps to his feet—*Is this it? The Big One?* he thinks. He stands in front of the fifty-two-inch TV screen, hopping back and forth, from one foot to the other, like a boxer in training. She remains seated on the couch, staring at him. They are both trying to remember what it is, exactly, that they're supposed to do when the big shaker hits. *Dive for cover? Stand in a doorway?* Forever that was the go-to advice, but he feels in recent years he has read reports that suggest it is maybe not the greatest spot to position yourself. All good so long as the lintel doesn't pop free and whack your head like a croquet ball. Either way, neither of them is exhibiting the best survival skills in the current situation. But luckily it is not the Big One, the one they say could take everything west of the I-5 and redraw the map of North America's West Coast. In reality it is a 6.5 off Tofino that does little to no damage.

Parking Meters

The VW van was loaded with camping gear and ready to go. They were now headed for the I-5, then the cut-off at Bellingham that would take them to the scenic route of Chuckanut Drive. Straight down the Washington and Oregon coast, en route, eventually, for Frisco, and then Carmel and Big Sur, the camperized van somehow climbing every incline thrown at it, including Neahkahnie Mountain and Cascade Head. And they will go visit the giant sequoia tree if things work out. Three days later they are crossing the Bay Bridge from Oakland to San Fran and merrily zooming toward North Beach and the city's historic Chinatown, where Melanie has secured them a room at a B&B on Post, or was it Kearny? He couldn't recall. Cheap and right in the heart of it. They will climb the nearly four hundred steps up the back of Coit Tower to take in the views before heading off for family-style Italian, then a jaunt to City Lights for the Beat vibe and a handful of books before crossing the alley (now Jack Kerouac Alley) to the legendary Vesuvio's to drink and review their literary acquisitions. Then wandering the streets through the cooling night air back toward Chinatown and their B&B. But they stop first for a nightcap, a cocktail to celebrate the day, to top off an excellent excursion, and when they come out and resume their walking—are they now on Grant? Maybe Stockton?—out the front of a walk-up and down the sidewalk, down the steep incline, shirtless and shoeless, comes a fit and furious specimen of a man carrying a fireman's axe. He is storming directly toward them and it would not be exaggerating to say they freeze in their steps, because they do exactly that. Brad thinks, *Wrong place, wrong time?* The guy who looks like he has stepped out of a firefighter's calendar stops about four car lengths away from them and lashes out at a parking meter, thrashing and shattering it with an axe designed to take out four-inch-thick wooden doors. Then he moves to the next meter, and a third, as the couple turns and heads the other way, looking over their shoulders to witness the strange occurrence unfolding on Grant, or Stockton, or maybe Post. Then Brad stops and grabs Melanie's hand, and she stops and turns too, and they watch the muscled back heading up the hill, axe swinging casually at the end of his right arm. They look at each other like they have just seen a lost spirit, or a unicorn, and for good measure they cross the street before continuing south to their B&B, and looking up, through the buildings, Brad catches a glimpse of Coit Tower and thinks of Lillie Hitchcock Coit, whose bequest to the city resulted in the tower's construction; she loved to chase fires in the early days of the city and respected the city's volunteer firefighters. Ms. Coit had a second bequest in her will, and that was to have a memorial built in honour of these firefighters, and that was done, and can be seen to this day in Washington Square.

She Said, He Said

He was having coffee around the corner from the old place. In what had been, for years, the Grind, but was now under new management with a theme of motorcycles and jazz. It was the spot where he had felt the *BANG!* of the 2001 6.8 Nisqually earthquake. As if an upright piano had been toppled in the adjacent room. Seismic. Like the wave of toxic masculinity he had hurled across the room and into her ear, killing the fetus. At least, that's what *she* said. It was, she said, he who had willed its heart to stop, to fail to thrive. Regardless, it, and everything else, died in that black moment, and washed away in the silent dark that followed. They could have named it but didn't. Hadn't. Maybe Hamlet—how many Hamlets have you met? Or Guinevere, or maybe Adolf—no, still too soon. Or something common—Lucy, Hannah, Paul—no, no Biblical references, please. The baby would be induced, she would go through labour and get nothing for it. Deliver death. The baby had checked out, decided, *No, not this time, not now.* Its potential to become, now uncoiling, unbecoming. And whatever *he* said, or *she* said, mattered not one iota. The baby was dead. Long-gone John. Dead. Gone.

Where We End Up

He tried to imagine himself dead. Corpse state, motionless on a slab—steel? Sheet metal? Marble? Would his mouth be gaping? Would he be naked, or would that come later? Would his fingers be clenched or relaxed? And the penis—shrunken and contracted to a stub or relaxed and hanging? Eyes: open to the ceiling, or closed, gently shut—as in the movies—by some attending medic? Would his hair, whiskers, fingernails, toenails continue to grow past his last breath, as is rumoured, and as may actually be, in fact, true, feeding on the body's proteins like a nurse stump? So many questions about death and a time he would never experience. Yet he knew all that was needed to be known. Wormed or burned, ashes or earth. In his case, on a small hill overlooking downtown, near the crypt of a city founder, a short distance from the crematorium, where one afternoon he had witnessed the soul of the deceased jettison from the short vent stack on the roof, moving at great speed amidst a mist of black particulate, westward, toward the Pacific Ocean and the blood-orange setting sun.

Acknowledgements

I would like to thank early readers of these pieces: Karen Green, Jane Silcott, TJ Beitelman, and Alban Goulden. I greatly appreciate your comments and insights; they have all served to make these pieces stronger. A huge thanks to my insightful and talented editor, Stuart Ross, for guiding the ship and keeping me off the shoals. And a big thanks to Fidel Peña of Underline Studio for the striking cover design. And to Laurie Siblock for her sharp proofreading.

Finally, I am extremely grateful to Michael Mirolla and Guernica Editions for providing a home for the 1366 Books imprint, and the rest of the team at Guernica, who have been wonderfully supportive and a joy to work with.

Plus, all the Mount Pleasant coffee shops and baristas that provided the necessary fuel to keep the engine running: Foglifter, Caffè Artigiano, Continental, Aperture, Forecast, 49th Parallel, JJBean, Coffee Date, Le Marché St. George, Matchstick (RIP)—you are all complicit in the creation of these stories.

Earlier versions of some of these pieces appeared in *subTerrain* magazine. I would also like to acknowledge the work of Diane Williams, Joy Williams, and Thomas Bernhard as inspiration for this project.

Nota bene: Many names in these stories have been changed to protect the guilty.

Brian Kaufman writes fiction, poetry, memoir, and drama. He has ushered over 250 Anvil Press books and 103 issues of *subTerrain* magazine into print since 1988. In 2009, Brian received the City of Vancouver's Mayor's Arts Award for his "significant contribution to Vancouver's arts and cultural community, for shaping Vancouver as a creative city, and for enriching the lives of Vancouver's citizens." He lives in what is called "Vancouver" on the ancestral and unceded land of the Coast Salish people. *Cascadia Subduction Shift* is his debut collection of fiction.

About 1366 Books

1366 Books is an imprint of Guernica Editions, launched in 2024 to bring to light two books of innovative but accessible fiction annually. Each title—whether a novel, stories, or microfictions—is a unique literary experience. Imprint editor Stuart Ross welcomes submissions of fiction manuscripts that challenge or attempt to redefine the boundaries of the genre. He is especially interested in seeing manuscripts of experimental fiction from members of diverse and marginalized communities. Write to Stuart at 1366books@gmail.com.

2024 *The Apple in the Orchard,* by Brian Dedora
Strange Water, by Sarah Moses

2025 *Furthermore, the Lake,* by Michael e. Casteels
A Mouth of Vowels, by Sophie Anne Edwards

2026 *Write Back Now!,* by Lisa Fishman
Cascadia Subduction Shift, by Brian Kaufman

1366Books

Exploding Fictions

MIX
Paper
FSC® C100212

Printed by Imprimerie Gauvin
Gatineau, Québec